"Think you might want to nanny some?"

"Timber and Sophia?"

He nodded. "You've probably noticed, my folks and I sort of share custody. They're happy to do it but they get tired, you know. And they're busy. But I can't manage the kids on my own, not while running my ministry."

She nodded. "So you want my help."

"If it wouldn't be too much trouble."

"Spend more time with my niece and nephew? I'd love it. Do you need to talk this over with the kids' social worker?"

"Already did. She said she ran a background check on you a couple days ago?"

She nodded. "When would you like me to start?"

"Would Monday morning be too soon?"

"Nope. Sounds perfect."

"Good. Thank you." He grabbed her hand again, twined his fingers quiet, peaceful mo becoming more de tight to. If only he make her stay.

Her nannying for him was a start.

Jennifer Slattery is a writer and speaker who has addressed women's and church groups across the nation. As the founder of Wholly Loved Ministries, she and her team help women rest in their true worth and live with maximum impact. When not writing, Jennifer loves spending time with her adult daughter and hilarious husband. Visit her online at jenniferslatterylivesoutloud.com to learn more or to book her for your next women's event.

Books by Jennifer Slattery

Love Inspired

Restoring Her Faith
Hometown Healing
Building a Family

Visit the Author Profile page at Harlequin.com.

Building a Family

Jennifer Slattery

LOVE INSPIRED
INSPIRATIONAL ROMANCE

LOVE INSPIRED®
INSPIRATIONAL ROMANCE

PLEASE RECYCLE — THIS PRODUCT IS RECYCLABLE

Recycling programs for this product may not exist in your area.

ISBN-13: 978-1-335-48822-0

Building a Family

Copyright © 2020 by Jennifer Slattery

This edition published by arrangement with Harlequin Books S.A.

For questions and comments about the quality of this book, please contact us at CustomerService@Harlequin.com.

Love Inspired
22 Adelaide St. West, 40th Floor
Toronto, Ontario M5H 4E3, Canada
www.Harlequin.com

Printed in U.S.A.

Can a woman forget her sucking child,
that she should not have compassion
on the son of her womb? yea, they may forget,
yet will I not forget thee. Behold, I have graven
thee upon the palms of my hands;
thy walls are continually before me.
—*Isaiah* 49:15–16

Dedicated to all those who consistently
speak life and hope into other people's lives.

Acknowledgments

I'm always amazed and so very grateful
to all the people God brings to help me
take a book from initial idea to print.
Though I couldn't possibly name them all,
there are those I would like to publicly thank.

First, my husband, who was the first to see
the emerging writer within me and call it out,
then spent the rest of our marriage encouraging
me to pursue my gift. I also want to thank
Doug Valentine, a Nebraska police officer,
for patiently and thoroughly answering
countless law-related questions. Then there's
my sweet friend LaShawn Montoya and
amazing critique partner Kristi Woods,
both of whom showed incredible reading skills
and a servant's heart to read the
revised version of this story in under a week.

Finally, I wanted to thank my sweet agent,
Tamela Hancock Murray. You are such a
treasure! Your heart for Jesus and your
continued support have meant the world to me!

Chapter One

Kayla Fisher wasn't one to invite conflict, yet here she sat, in Noah Williams's gravel driveway, about to initiate a conversation certain to be anything but pleasant.

A handful of vehicles, predominantly rusted trucks, filled the small gravel lot. She eyed the scalloped-edge main ranch house in front of her, with peeling paint and a covered porch. Was this the right place? She checked the address scrawled on the notepad beside her then glanced about. To her left, maybe a hundred yards away on the same property, sat a gray mobile home with blue trim. Some distance beyond, at three o'clock, stood a faded red barn, fenced corral and what appeared to be stables.

Kayla sent Trista, her longest-lasting and dearest friend, a text. I'm here. Pray for me. And for my niece and nephew.

Kayla's sister still hadn't replied to all the frantic messages she had sent her. *Christy, where are you?* Something had to be wrong, because the alternative—that she'd completely abandoned her children, a toddler and infant—was incomprehensible.

What type of mother could do that?

One who was using again, that was who.

Lord, show me what to do here. Kayla wasn't prepared to take on the role of motherhood. Her interior-design firm was just starting to gain traction. Besides, her hours were long and often unpredictable. Children needed stability, someone with more availability. A husband wouldn't hurt, either. But Kayla couldn't allow the state to place her niece and nephew into foster care.

Would Noah Williams, their daddy's brother, want to raise them? Surely the former bull rider, who'd once earned the title of Sage Creek's biggest partier, wasn't any more ready to play parent than she was. With all his girl-chasing, bar-hopping…

No. She was her niece and nephew's best option.

She eyed her reflection in the rearview mirror, her red eyes evidence of her lack of sleep. Her auburn locks hung limp, hitting just below her chin. After a long day of travel, exhaustion and anxiety had paled her normally rosy complexion.

And she had a feeling that whatever she was stepping into was just beginning.

She exited her vehicle and breathed in the humid Texas air, the familiar scent of earth and hay offering some comfort.

Gravel crunched beneath her as she strode toward the lopsided stairs leading to the ranch-house entrance. She stopped on the covered porch to bolster her courage, then knocked.

A moment later the door opened to reveal a short, apple-shaped woman with long blond hair parted down the center. She held baby Sophia, who was squirming and fussing, in her arms. In a far corner, Kayla's nephew, Timber, was stacking plastic cups one on top of the other.

"Hello." The woman offered a wide smile, though she was clearly frazzled. She looked to be in her midfifties. "How may I help you?"

Kayla introduced herself and smoothed a hand over Sophia's soft head. "I'm here to see Noah. And my precious niece and nephew." She crossed the room to where Timber was playing. "Hey, buddy." She moved to hug him, but he shied away, as if he'd forgotten who she was.

Had it been that long since she'd last seen him?

"Noah's leading a class right now."

"We have an appointment."

The woman wiggled a paper calendar out from under an overstuffed diaper bag. With Sophia balanced on her hip, she flipped through some pages. "You're a day early."

"Are you sure?" Kayla felt certain she'd told Noah she'd be coming into town today. She'd scrambled to get the earliest flight she could afford and had rearranged her rather full schedule to make this happen.

Sophia began to cry, and the woman started to bounce her. "No matter. I'm sure he can step away for a moment." She picked up a phone and tapped the screen. "Kayla Fisher is here to see you." She paused. "Okay. I'll show her back."

She gave Timber a stern eye. "You be good and stay right where you're at."

If he heard her, he gave no indication.

"Follow me." She led Kayla down a dimly lit hall, past a cluttered office barely bigger than a storage closet, through a galley kitchen and out the back. They continued to a barn filled with various band saws and other machines manned by a smattering of men, one dressed in coveralls, the others in jeans, flannels and T-shirts. At least half of them had thick beards, long hair and large tattooed arms.

Sawdust and wood shavings covered the ground, while shelves lined with branches, planks and stumps stood above a cluster of chairs and bar stools. The scents of cedar, earth and varnish tickled Kayla's nose.

She recognized Noah's six-foot-plus, broad-shouldered frame instantly. He wore faded jeans and gray boots, and the tips of his ash-brown hair curled out from beneath his Stetson. He was as muscular as she remembered, if not more so. The scruff of a beard he'd developed in high school had filled out, and he now wore it trimmed and neat.

She'd once had quite a crush on him. Before he'd turned wild and reckless.

He appeared to be engaged in a tense conversation with an angry-looking teen with longish black hair that swooped to the side.

The woman watched the two with her hands clasped in front of her. Finally, she stepped forward. "Noah, Kayla Fisher is here to see you."

Noah turned in their direction, his green-gray eyes making Kayla's breath catch.

The kid Noah was talking to started to leave. Noah grabbed his arm.

The teen jerked back. "Dude. Lay off." He stormed away, and the woman called after him.

"Let him go, Brenda." Noah stepped closer. "Give him a minute to cool off." He tipped his Stetson at Kayla and looped a thumb through his belt. "Thanks for coming out on such short notice."

"Absolutely."

He studied her as if gauging what to say, or maybe what not to say. "Mind if we talk somewhere quieter?"

She swallowed and nodded, then followed him back the way she'd come, finally to a kitchen table covered with forms and brochures. She looked at the front of one—Helping Hands Ministry: Using Craftsmanship to Rebuild Lives. A phone number and address followed.

She met his gaze. "This what you do?"

He nodded. "We help men beat their addictions by teaching them to make something useful. Something they can be proud of so that maybe they'll man up and stop self-destructing."

A framed newspaper clipping hung on the wall behind him, with a photo of him standing in his barn-turned-workshop, two other men on either side. The headline read, Former Bull Rider Stands Among Us as One Who Serves. Next to this hung an image of an eagle soaring above a mountainous landscape, with the words:

If the Son therefore shall make you free, ye shall be free indeed. John 8:36.

"How was your trip?" Noah asked.

Whether he was practicing the Southern hospitality Sage Creek was known for or was asking to give her time to compose herself, she was grateful. "Uneventful."

"Good. I hear you've been doing well. Started your own business, making a name for yourself in the interior-design world."

She shrugged. "Working on it." In fact, up until she'd received the call about her sister, she'd been preparing for the Pacific Northwest Home Designs Tour, one of the most prestigious home shows in the nation. At this moment, the local television crews and newspaper reporters were likely interviewing her competitors in preparation for the big reveals. A designer could really make a name for herself through that event.

Hopefully Kayla's assistant had managed to snag some camera time.

"I know this is hard." The tenderness in Noah's voice squeezed her heart. "Unexpected."

She nodded. "So what now?"

"I'm still trying to figure all that out. When did you last hear from your sister?"

Kayla winced inwardly as guilt pricked her. She should've checked on her more, visited more. Then maybe she would've noticed when Christy had started slipping. If that was what had occurred. "It's been a while. She's not one to text or talk on the phone."

"Haven't seen or heard hide or tail of my brother, either. Not in a long time."

That Kayla knew. Christy had been raising Timber by herself since before Sophia was born. Largely from the get-go, actually. "My sister loves those kids. I can't believe…" She swallowed. "Do you think something happened?"

Noah looked at her for an extended moment, then shook his head. "I wish I could say yes. But—you know how gossip travels here—word has it she's been spending time in the bars again. Hanging out with her old crew." His phone chimed. He glanced at the screen then set it on the table. "How long you in town for?"

She released a breath and raked a hand through her hair. "As long as I need to be."

He rubbed his thumb knuckle. "The kids got a home here. They've formed relationships. At church, with my parents." A tendon in his jaw twitched. "With me."

"Meaning?"

"They've experienced enough upheaval as it is."

Was he saying he planned to keep them? For how long? That eased some of the pressure off her, but was that best? Surely he knew less about parenting than she did, especially considering his upbringing, if all the rumors circulating around Sage Creek had been true. Granted, his mom left her abusive husband prior to moving here, but not before Noah had witnessed his fair share of violence, or so she'd heard.

Everyone said his background contributed to his tenacity and courage as a bull rider. But those traits that gained him rodeo victories could easily work against him when it came to dealing with crying babies and headstrong toddlers.

He studied her. "How much do you know?"

"About what happened?"

He nodded.

"News travels in Sage Creek." Not that Kayla accepted church gossip as fact. At least, she hoped the accounts she'd heard weren't true. She'd received a voice mail from a woman claiming to be the children's social worker but hadn't managed to connect with her yet.

"Billy Johnson was out making his trash rounds. Said he found Timber just after seven in the morning wandering out on the gravel road about half a mile from Christy's place. Billy scooped him up and drove him home." Noah exhaled. "Found quite a mess. Empty liquor bottles and trash everywhere. Place colder than an icebox, no food except half a jar of mayonnaise in the fridge. And poor little Sophia…" He shook his head. "So Billy called the cops, they contacted Child Protective Services and, as far as I know, no one's seen or heard of your sister since."

Now what? Hopefully the social worker would call Kayla back soon, explain what the next steps were.

What if she asked Kayla to take the kids? Was she prepared for that?

"I'm staying at the Cedar View Inn just outside of town." She sat taller. "I'd like to bring Timber and Sophia with me."

"Why?"

"What do you mean?"

"Move these kids to a hotel when they've got a perfectly fine place to stay right here with me?"

"Timber, get off of that!" Brenda's sharp voice emanated from the other room. What sounded like a toddler-size fit followed.

Kayla arched an eyebrow and faced Noah. "Seems to me y'all could use some help."

He held her gaze while the ruckus in the other room continued. Was he challenging her? It felt as if *she* was challenging him. Maybe she was. But she knew little about this man, his temperament or his parenting skills.

Why hadn't he said anything? Surely he'd seen Christy falling back into her old behavior. Maybe if he'd stepped in to help, acted like a loving and involved uncle, they wouldn't be in this situation now.

Noah gave a quick nod. "All right. You should come to my parents' place for dinner tonight. I'd like my mom to be included in these discussions. We'd welcome a hand, I'm sure, if that's what you're offering. So long as you're in town."

"Oh, I don't plan on going anywhere, Mr. Williams." At least, not until she knew the children were well cared for.

Noah walked Kayla out, closed the door behind her and released a heavy breath.

"What're you going to do?" Brenda asked.

"About Christy's sister?"

What if she fought for custody of the kids? She probably felt she'd do a better job minding them, being a woman and all. But that'd kill his parents, his mom especially. She loved being a grandma and had grown mighty attached to those little ones. If not for his stepdad's early onset Alzheimer's, which kept his mom busy, they'd be the best candidates to adopt Timber and Sophia themselves.

Maybe *they* couldn't, but Noah sure could. And run his ministry? He'd just have to make it work, get help from the community when necessary. That was how they did things in Sage Creek. Everyone banded together, and they would rally around him for this. He certainly had more right to those children than Kayla, who lived five states away and popped in maybe twice a year.

Brenda crossed her arms. "I'm asking how you plan to handle our angry community-service friend who went barreling out of here faster than a hound after a raccoon."

"Anyone come to pick him up?"

She shook her head.

"Then he'll be back." The kid hadn't been the first assigned to serve at Helping Hands only to leave in a huff. Too bad he threw his little fit on the day Kayla came, though. Might color the way she saw this place, which could cause problems later.

"That teen's sense will return once he realizes how many miles are between us and town. If he can't handle a bit of woodworking, then he for sure won't make it far on foot. When he comes back, give him a tuna sandwich and a Coke and call his mama to come get him. Remind them both of our rules and expectations."

"And that pretty little thing with the cute auburn-streaked bob?"

He smiled. Kayla had always been beautiful. Even more so now, standing at maybe five foot on her best day.

She also, potentially, had the power to snatch his niece and nephew right out of his hands. "I invited her to dinner at my folks' place."

Brenda raised an eyebrow.

"I suspect we'll have to find a way to work together. For the sake of the kids. And so long as she understands they're staying in Sage Creek, we'll get along just fine."

The ministry's doorbell rang. Brenda answered it to find the mailman standing on the stoop. "Noah Williams?"

"That's me." Noah stepped forward and the man handed him an electronic tablet.

"Sign here, please."

Noah complied and was handed a letter from the county. After the man left, he opened it up, read it, blinked, then read it again.

"What is it?" Brenda peered over his shoulder.

"We're being sued."

"What? For what?"

This couldn't be happening. Not now. "Seems Ralph— You remember him?"

She nodded. "The heavyset rancher with the foul mouth and hostile disposition."

"That's the one." Brenda had warned Noah not to hire the guy, and he hadn't lasted two months. He'd been argumentative and called in sick at least one day a week, and Noah suspected he'd been stealing supplies. "He's claiming wrongful termination. Age discrimination."

"We've got proof that says otherwise. You documented your one-on-ones with him, right?"

"Most of them. Regardless, we don't have funds for a legal suit right now." Or ever. They were barely making ends meet as it was.

"What're you going to do?"

Timber ran across the room with his arms outstretched, squealing like a strangled donkey.

Noah would've laughed if he hadn't been so stressed.

"Think you can do some calling around to find us a good lawyer…that we can afford?"

"Where are we going to get funds for that?"

He exhaled and scrubbed a hand over his face. "We'll figure it out."

He grabbed Timber by the waist as he made a second loop around, tossed him over his shoulder and tickled his ribs. "I got to corral the rascals to head out, and try to beat Kayla to my folks' place." Right now, the children needed his full focus. He had to trust God with the rest.

He had to believe God would come through somehow, because he just couldn't lose his ministry. Too many men, a handful of whom were still in the early phase of recovery, were counting on him, as were their families.

He and the children arrived at his parents' to find all three adults gathered in the living room over sweet tea and cookies. Kayla and his mom were talking while his stepdad stared aimlessly straight ahead. He'd taken to doing that more and more lately.

"Sorry I'm late getting here." Noah set his Stetson on an entryway table. The rich aroma of garlic and roasted beef wafted toward him. "I got caught behind a train just east of town. Did you all solve world hunger while waiting for me?"

Kayla met Noah's eye, and a slight blush colored her cheeks. She was even more beautiful than he remembered—pretty enough to jumble a man's head, if he let her.

"Seems we worked ourselves into a bit of a tangle, if anything." Mom dropped her gaze, but then she brightened and turned to Timber. "How's Grandma's hunka-hunka?" She gave Timber a squeeze then positioned him on her lap. "Were you good for Uncle Noah and Miss Brenda?"

Timber nodded. "Chocwate puddin'?"

Noah's mom laughed. "After dinner, maybe. If you eat all your carrots."

Timber wrinkled his nose, eliciting more laughter, then wiggled his way to the floor. He immediately migrated to Noah's old toy box, which his mom had saved. That was an indication of just how long she'd dreamed of being a grandmother. Grieving her husband's deteriorating mental state as she was, she needed every drop of joy these little ones brought.

Surely Kayla could see that, though he couldn't tell much from her guarded expression.

The dinner conversation proved more awkward than Noah had anticipated. Clearly staking her territory, his mom talked about all the wonderful activities Timber was involved with, how attached he'd become to the nursery workers at church and how much he just adored Noah. Meanwhile, Kayla kept her responses short and her eye on Noah's stepdad, almost as if analyzing his behavior or mental state.

Either that or maybe she was just in shock, not that he'd blame her. He was still trying to process it all himself.

He caught her eye and offered what he hoped was a reassuring smile. "The kids are lucky you're here. Together—" he motioned to indicate her and his mom "—we'll make sure these kids receive every ounce of love and care they deserve and then some."

Chapter Two

After dinner, Timber seemed wound up, so Noah suggested they take him outside to play. "Might give the two of you some time to reconnect, on his turf."

Kayla nodded, fighting what was becoming a familiar surge of guilt for not having been more involved. Not just when Christy became a mom, but even before, like after the deaths of their parents. Kayla had seen the signs, even back then. Her sister had started hanging out with some sketchy kids, going to parties, acting flirty with older guys. But Kayla had been too caught up in her own grief—and with going to college, then chasing after her career—to intervene.

Was it too late now?

Maybe to save her sister, but not her sister's kids. She'd do right by them; she owed Christy and their parents that much.

Noah squatted in front of his nephew and managed to slow down the tyke long enough to put on his sandals. "Don't know why I bother, seeing how he'll kick these off before his feet hit the grass."

He shot Kayla a wink that threatened to turn her insides to mush.

"All right, Timber Tonka. Let's see if we can't wear some of your wiggles out before bedtime." He lifted the boy by his arms and deposited him on his feet. "You got the princess?"

She nodded, suddenly unable to voice coherent words.

It was probably due to the tumultuous emotions that had hit her ever since she'd learned of her niece and nephew's abandonment. Her brain freeze certainly had nothing to do with the handsome, muscular man who was, at this moment, watching her much too intently.

It was as if he was trying to figure her out, though a hint of kindness shone through his green-gray eyes.

"Ladies first." He brushed his knuckles against Sophia's cheek then held the door open for them.

"Thank you." Kayla stepped onto the porch. Timber made a vrooming noise and dashed past her with his fist raised in front of him. He toddled toward the sidewalk and the street beyond.

Noah descended the steps two at a time, swept up the little one, tossed him in the air a couple of times, then carried him to a bucket swing hanging from an old oak tree centered in the lawn. "Got to keep a close eye on this one."

"I can see that."

Kayla followed and sat in a wooden Adirondack chair positioned in the shade.

Noah gave Timber a gentle push. "How do you like northern Washington? Does it really rain as much as everyone says?"

"More." She smiled.

"You miss Sage Creek?"

She watched a girl in braids pedal by on a pink bike with glittery handlebar tassels. A woman in running gear jogged half a pace behind. "The people, sometimes." But this was also a place that reminded her of pain, of the day she'd learned of her parents' deaths.

"How about the church potlucks?"

She laughed. "Those, too."

"So why'd you leave?"

"To chase my dream. I knew I'd never be able to support myself in Sage Creek as an interior designer."

The sun dipped lower on the horizon, painting the sky in streaks of pink and violet. A car drove by, and families started trickling out of their homes, some to play catch in the yard, others to walk their dogs.

"Have you heard from JD at all?" she asked.

He shook his head. "My brother abandoned those kids the moment your sister first got pregnant. He'd pop in for a day or two, play family, then leave. At least, that's what it looked like from where I sat. My parents tried talking to him a few times, but he never listened. Then, once little Sophia came along, he left for good."

She nodded. She knew all that. Christy had complained about Noah's brother often enough. Kayla had listened and always been indignant, telling her sister how she didn't deserve such treatment and needed to leave the "lying, cheating, irresponsible loser." Now her sister was acting just like him.

Maybe she had been all along.

Noah plucked a blade of grass from the lawn. "Look, I know this feels crazy hard now, and probably confusing, too. But everything will work out. I truly believe that."

She wanted to believe that, too, but her heart refused to settle until she knew where her sister was, that she was okay and that Timber and Sophia were, too.

She studied him for a long moment. "What's your work schedule like?"

"You asking if I have time to take care of the kids?"

She gave a one-shoulder shrug. Her question might seem harsh, but she needed to know.

"My mom stays pretty involved, as she can. We come for dinner a few evenings a week, give or take. Some of the quilting ladies from church help out on occasion, when I need an extra hand. Other than that, they come to work with me, and Brenda, my assistant, keeps an eye on them."

"That doesn't concern you, all that shuffling from one person to the next?" Then again, she'd probably have to do the same, should the children move in with her. Only she'd probably get a nanny.

"Why should it?"

"What about with your dad?" She could tell something wasn't right with him. Surely that added stress to the situation.

"I'm not concerned."

"I hope you don't mind me asking, but when did your parents get back together?"

His brow furrowed. "Wait. Did you think Ben, my mom's husband, was my bio dad? The jerk who used to beat us?"

"He's not?"

He shook his head, chuckling.

"But you called them your parents."

He nodded. "That man in there is the closest thing to a father I've had. Earned that name through lots of prayers and holding tight to me when I was nothing but a source of continual pain. He helped me turn my life around when I was heading straight for an early grave. On more than one occasion, and not just counting all the times I was tossed off an angry bull or kicked or stepped on."

"Oh." Her tense shoulders relaxed. "That's good to hear."

"You can't seriously think I'd put my niece and nephew in harm's way."

"Sometimes hopeful thinking distorts our perception." The irony of her statement, in light of her history with her sister, stung. "Listen, I'd love to help. At least, while I'm here. I know it can't be easy, playing the daddy role while running your ministry and all."

He studied her then gave a slow nod. "I appreciate it. Think that'd be good for the kids, too, but that's not really a choice I can make."

"What do you mean? Whose choice is it?"

"The kids are technically wards of the state, which means whoever they stay with, whether that's for an afternoon or an overnight, needs to have a background check done."

"You included?"

"Yep. I had to jump through all the hoops just like everyone else. I'm sort of acting as their foster parent."

"But you're their uncle."

"That, too." He smiled. "The folks from Child Protective Services have a certain way of doing things, you know?"

"Okay. So what do I need to do?"

"I'll talk to their social worker, have her contact you with next steps."

"She left me a voice mail. I called her back but haven't heard from her yet."

"S'pect she's a mite busy. Word has it she handles all the county's CPS cases. Plus, she's been out of town." He scratched his jaw. "In the meantime, we can keep getting together, so you can see the kids."

She sighed.

His eyes softened. "Look, I know this is frustrating."

"It is, though none of this is your fault." Not that that made the whole situation any easier. Suddenly, her phone pinged. She checked her screen, then exhaled. It was her assistant, not her sister. You're not going to believe who just phoned us for an estimate. John Kollings.

She texted back: Seriously???? For what?

Her assistant texted, A complete remodel of his downtown law firm, maybe one in Blair, too.

Kayla needed to be there. There was no way Nicole could schmooze such a high-dollar client, and who knew how many others would follow before the home show concluded. This was business they desperately needed if they wanted to remain competitive in Bellingham's changing market.

But she also needed to be here. She abandoned her sister, back when she'd needed her most. She refused to do the same to Timber and Sophia.

Chapter Three

The next morning, Kayla went to the library to use their Wi-Fi. She had a video conference scheduled with a textile company from Seattle, and she didn't trust the spotty service at her hotel. She'd barely logged on when her phone rang. It was Nicole.

"Hey, more good news, I hope," Kayla said as she opened her email.

"Um. Not exactly. I just got a call from Mrs. Finnerty."

Kayla groaned. "What now?" That woman was about as moody as a sleep-deprived middle schooler. Kayla would cut her loose if not for the fact that her custom-designed residence was what had gotten them into the home show…and was scheduled to appear on television in less than two weeks. To make matters worse, they'd invested a lot of money into the project, content to trade profits for the promotional opportunity.

"She fired the tile guy."

A jolt of adrenaline cramped her gut. "You cannot be serious."

"I wish I were joking."

"What happened?"

"I wasn't there, but apparently he started putting in the tile and she said she didn't like it. That it was too yellow."

"But she picked it out."

"I'm just telling you what she said. She accused Riley of ordering cheap material."

"He had nothing to do with that."

"Regardless, things turned heated. She called him names I'd rather not repeat and sent him packing."

Kayla rubbed her face. Now what? "Any chance you can smooth things over?"

"I've tried."

"Call Jeoffry Maynard. Ask if he can finish the job. I'll call Mrs. Finnerty, see if I can't get her to change her mind regarding the tile, or else maybe talk her into ordering a stone with less color variation." Fortunately, she wanted her home to appear in the home show as much as Kayla did, and would therefore be motivated to compromise. At least, that was Kayla's hope.

Nicole sighed. "At this point, I'd say she hates about everything we've done."

"She's probably just nervous, thinking about all the media coverage."

"Maybe."

"I say we do whatever we have to in order to finish this project and move on." And quickly. "We might lose a bit on this one, but with all the estimates you copied me on, seems we should be able to make up any potential deficit and then some." So long as Nicole handled everything right and they didn't have any more major issues while Kayla was in Texas.

"Sorry." Nicole sounded defeated.

"Don't let this stress you out. Consider it training for when we land those Seattle millionaire clients we keep dreaming about."

Nicole gave a weak laugh. "Okay." Paper rustled on the other end.

"Anything else?"

"Actually, yeah. You know the wine-colored paint we ordered for the Ansels?"

"Yes?" Their biggest job of the year, outside of the Finnertys. Of course she remembered.

"It's pink."

"What?"

"The paint. Mrs. Ansel just called. She's pretty upset."

"So have the guys swing through the hardware store. That shouldn't set us back but a couple hours."

"The wall's already covered, floor to ceiling, and apparently Mr. Ansel cut his business trip early and is heading home."

"Okay." That didn't sound insurmountable. They'd be out whatever extra wages it cost to have the painters redo the job, but that wouldn't hurt them too much.

"According to his wife, he didn't know she'd hired us."

"What?" Note to self: from now on, when a project involved more than one homeowner, Nicole should insist both parties sign off on it.

"I feel like I'm really blowing it." Nicole sounded on the verge of tears.

"These things happen." Though not normally back-to-back like this, and during such an important season. "We'll get through this."

The glass doors beside her swooshed open, and a familiar deep voice made her breath stall.

"Remember our story-time rules."

She turned to see Noah walking in holding Timber's chubby hand. He grinned and tipped his hat at her.

She smiled to hide the jittery feeling that swept through her, then straightened. What was it about that man that set her off-kilter? She refocused on her phone call. "All we can do is fix the situation as best we can. We're not responsible for Mrs. Ansel's deceptive behavior. Nor do we have any control over how she or her husband respond."

Timber eyed her, lagging behind his uncle.

Kayla waved, and he lurched forward and hugged Noah's leg. Noah scooped him up and carried him over his shoulder, triggering that high-pitched giggle that melted her heart.

Though her phone call with Nicole tempted her to hurry home, she couldn't possibly leave now, not with so much left unsettled. She asked her assistant, "Is this something you feel you can handle?"

Nicole paused. "Sure. Yeah. No problem. You do your thing."

As if she was on some sort of vacation.

She pocketed her phone, then headed back inside to find Noah talking to the librarian while Timber was pulling books from the staff-favorites shelf. He held one out to her.

She dropped to his level. "Why, thank you." She glanced at the title and laughed. *"Easy, Guilt-Free Meals for Vegans."*

Noah joined them. "Ah. Looks like little man's about to go healthy. Is that right, Timber? You trading your chicken nuggets for celery?" The toddler resumed his book-grabbing-and-restacking game. Noah shifted to face Kayla, his gaze latching on to hers. "You sleep well?" The aqua in his snug T-shirt brought out a hint of blue in his eyes.

She swallowed to suppress the jittery feeling the man always seemed to trigger in her—a reaction he likely evoked in countless women. "Not too bad. You're not at work today?"

"I've been spending Fridays in town. Save my mornings for some one-on-one time with Timber. We always come to story time, don't we, bud?" He gave him a side squeeze. "Friday afternoons I run errands and attend meetings or whatnot." He moved aside, tipping his hat as two ladies walked past pushing toddlers in strollers. "Today's toddler story time."

She followed his gaze to the brightly decorated children's area, where a group of moms and little ones had gathered. Her heart warmed at the thought of Noah sitting among them, legs crossed on the floor, Timber on his lap.

"Come!" Timber tugged him forward.

Noah chuckled. "Hold up, buddy. We've got to clean up our mess first." He squatted to reshelf the books scattered on the floor.

Kayla helped. "Seems your uncle is planting the reading bug in you good and early." She ruffled her nephew's hair, pleased when he didn't shrink back. He was likely too focused on unshelving each book she and Noah had put back.

"Something like that."

Timber pushed against Noah's back with a whiny grunt, then took off toward the kids' section.

"You go." Kayla waved a hand. "I've got this."

"You sure?"

"Yep."

"Thanks." His boyish smile sent a wave of warmth through her. If she wasn't careful, her heart would become irreparably entangled.

Noah followed Timber to the story-time carpet—a large, circular rug decorated with animals, each in a different colored square. A large number of other children had already gathered, some sitting cross-legged beside their moms, others on laps.

"Come on, bud." Noah folded his long legs, feeling massive surrounded by petite ladies and their youngins. Like a bull in a pen of fillies. Timber sat on the ground and inched closer to his uncle, soon engrossed in the tread at the bottom of his shoes.

"Good morning, boys and girls!" Elsie Bennett, one of the librarians, sat between two large stuffed dolls on a long wooden bench. A polka-dot box waited at her feet, and she held a book in her hand. "Do you think Jimbo will come out to play today?"

Some of the older kids cheered, and numerous little ones inched forward.

"Let's call him now." She placed the box on her lap and peeked inside. "Jimbo, oh, Jimbo, won't you come out to play?" The adults and children joined her. "Jimbo, oh, Jimbo, it's story time today."

She reached inside the box then pulled out the familiar clown puppet. The children squealed, and Timber rocked back and forth, giggling. Noah gave him a sideways hug. What Noah wouldn't do to keep that boy smiling. There was no telling what Timber had experienced under Christy's care.

Rubbing the back of his hand beneath his beard, he glanced back toward Kayla to find her watching Timber with a look of longing, or maybe sorrow. When her gaze met his, pink tinged her cheeks.

She quickly averted her eyes back to the computer in front of her. He could tell by her body language she was brain-deep in something serious, likely related to Timber and Sophia.

Custody-type stuff?

What if Christy lost her parental rights and Kayla

stepped in, fought for the kids and took them back to Washington State? Or maybe to her grandparents in Houston?

Surely she wouldn't do that—uproot them from their community.

But the state could determine she was a better fit, being a female and all.

Would Kayla stand up for him and explain why the kids needed to stay in Sage Creek, or would she welcome the opportunity to take them? Surely she'd put them first.

He glanced back at her, immediately captivated by the way she tilted her head when in thought and how her eyes lit whenever they landed on her nephew.

"Are you ready for craft time?" Elsie's chipper voice redirected his thoughts.

He stood on stiff legs and followed the swarm of chattering children to a rectangular table covered in flower shapes cut from construction paper, glue sticks, stickers and doodads of various colors and shapes.

"Mine!" Timber snatched a marker from a little girl, and she began to cry.

Noah placed a gentle but firm hand on his nephew's forearm. "We don't take things from others, little man. Now give the marker back to your friend."

It took some prodding, but eventually Timber complied, and soon his hands and the table in front of him were covered with glue and paper bits. The end result was a conglomeration of green, gold, blue and red that, with a bit of imagination, resembled a summer garden.

An art project that would land prominently on Noah's fridge.

Unless… Maybe he should encourage Timber to give his creation to Kayla, to help the two of them build a relationship. She was his aunt, after all, and she clearly cared for him.

He didn't trust her to take the kiddos by herself for fear she'd bring them straight to Christy. But that didn't mean he couldn't invite her to join him for things. Like story time or park days.

He glanced back to where she'd been sitting. An older woman with puffy silver hair occupied the table where Kayla had been, and a quick scan of the library indicated she'd left. To head back to her hotel?

He glanced at the time on his phone. More likely was grabbing a bite at Wilma's Café. Which reminded him, he had a lunch meeting at the church to get to.

He'd catch Kayla tomorrow, see if they couldn't work something out.

For the children's sake.

Course, spending time with that golden-eyed beauty wouldn't hurt him none.

But thinking that way—about Kayla—would only tangle his mind, when he needed to be as clearheaded as possible.

Chapter Four

Saturday morning, Noah met with his ministry board members over coffee. He'd made copies of all the documents related to the situation with Ralph, along with Brenda's estimation of legal fees. "Lawyers from our county have the best rates." He made a star by one firm he recognized and had heard some good things about.

"But the lawyers from Houston and Austin have more experience with this sort of thing." Terrance, his treasurer, flipped over one page and started reading the next.

"And their price reflects that." Noah glanced at their financials. Where were they going to find the money for a retainer, let alone to win the lawsuit?

Elliot tapped his pen in his hand. "There's no way this guy will win."

"Even so, this is still going to cost us a pretty penny." Maybe even enough to put them under. He rubbed the back of his neck, calculating the value of their inventory. "We're lower than normal on merchandise. We've had a lot of new guys come in, some with zero carpentry skills and a lot of emotional needs. They're learning, for sure, but it's been slow going as we try to balance their woodworking lessons with our recovery programs."

Elliot nodded. "Two of our guys have spent a lot more time in our anger-management class and group therapy than on our shop floor."

"All right…" Terrance flipped to a clean sheet on his yellow pad. "If we were to liquidate all our furniture in stock…" He punched numbers into his calculator. "We can earn just shy of fifteen thousand dollars, maybe twenty thousand. That should be enough to get us started."

"We'd need to replenish and sell nearly the equivalent pretty quickly in order to make budget." Noah made a mental list of upcoming craft shows. If only they could get hired on for another remodel, like they had with Drake Owens and his grandmother's dinner theater a few years back. At the time, he hadn't known Drake all that well, though he remembered his name from high school. But then one day he and his girlfriend, who later became his wife, showed up at Noah's ministry asking for the largest order Helping Hands had had to date. That'd stretched them, for sure, but it'd also provided a huge financial payoff.

Wait. What type of interior designing did Kayla do? Might be a long shot to hope she'd need anything for any current projects she was working on. But maybe she had leads he could follow up on, like a hotel-lobby remodel or something.

What were the odds she'd know anyone who wanted rustic furniture made from refurbished wood? Still, it was worth a try.

He tidied his papers into a stack. "We've got this. Scratch that. *God's* got this. He's been carrying this ministry since I launched it. He's not going to let us fail now."

"Amen." Elliot slapped a hand on the table. "Because we've still got too much to do, too many lives to change and addictions to break, to let a liar like Ralph shut us down."

Elliot checked the time on his phone and stood. "I'll make some calls, see if I can't drum up more sales outlets. Terrance, can you meet with prospective lawyers, find out their background, experience and qualifications, and get their thoughts on the case?"

Terrance nodded, and everyone gathered their things and left. Noah called Kayla on the way to his truck.

"Hi." The enthusiasm in her voice made him smile. "Everything okay?"

"Yep. I was actually calling for business reasons." He climbed into his cab and turned on the engine. The twang of a banjo poured from his speakers. He turned off his radio. "Think maybe we could meet? To talk interior-design stuff?"

"Um, sure. When were you thinking?"

"When are you available?"

She hesitated. "Maybe this afternoon? I'm heading over to Christy's right now."

A jolt shot through him, and his grip tightened on the phone. "She's back?"

Kayla sighed. "No. At least, I don't think so. But I told my grandparents I'd stop by to check and nose about, see if I can get any hints as to where she might be."

"Oh." That had to be killing them. He knew what that felt like. "Mind if I stop by? My mom's been asking me to look for Timber's and Sophia's immunization records." Assuming they existed. "So we can register him for pre-school this spring."

"Sure. I guess. Though I have to warn you, I'm not in the most cheerful mood."

"No problem. I understand." And he did. More than she knew.

* * *

After all the gossip involving her sister, Kayla thought she'd prepared herself mentally and emotionally for what she might find once she arrived at her house. She hadn't. Seeing all the empty liquor bottles lying around her sister's place broke her heart. Even if Christy came back, she had no business raising those kids. At least, not until she received serious help, like rehab.

Kayla had an urge to call Noah, which was silly, and not just because he'd be arriving soon enough. Whenever they interacted, he seemed so calm and levelheaded, while she felt anything but. His demeanor and steady confidence had a way of soothing her. Besides, they were basically in this together. If they lived closer, maybe they could even rear the children as a team.

An image of the two of them, sitting on a park bench, Sophia asleep in her arms and Timber playing in the sand, came to mind, and her heart squeezed.

She'd always discarded the idea of marriage, of having a family, mainly because of her career. And that hadn't changed. She couldn't run a successful, growing design firm while playing soccer mom.

Could she?

Not from Sage Creek, and there was no way Noah would move to the West Coast. Which meant she either needed to relinquish the children to his care or fight him for custody. Neither option felt appealing.

If only Mama and Daddy were still alive, none of this would've happened.

A box filled with what appeared to be picture albums and momentos sat near her sister's unmade bed.

Kayla uncovered a yearbook near the bottom that was dated the year before her graduation. She'd been a junior, Christy a freshman.

She flipped to the baseball-team pages and found a picture of Noah. He'd been a senior and stood half a foot taller than his teammates, and was the most muscular among them. Back then his hair was longer, and he always seemed to wear a smirk.

She hadn't seen that cocky expression once since she'd arrived in Sage Creek. Seemed he'd traded it for a gentle, easy smile, one that managed to calm and unsettle her simultaneously.

Car tires crunched on the gravel drive.

Christy?

She dashed to the door and looked out. Noah, wearing his signature Stetson and a checked shirt. Her heart simultaneously sank and leaped as disappointment that it wasn't her sister collided with the joy of seeing Noah.

She straightened and took in a slow breath, willing logic to override her clearly rebellious emotions. She was here to see after the children, not fall for a handsome cowboy with a rough past.

Noah tipped his hat at her and climbed the steps. "Morning." He looked past her into the house, then back to her. "Any success?"

"What?"

"Figuring out where your sister took off to?"

"Oh. No."

He studied her for a long moment, his eyes searching hers. "Want to talk about it?"

She sat, her back pressed against the railing slats, and hugged her knees. He joined her, his presence calming her frazzled emotions.

She watched lazy puffs of clouds drift across the horizon. "When we were kids, my parents used to call Christy their little firecracker. She was always moving and looking to have fun. Chasing one crazy idea after another."

"Like what?"

"Christy loved dandelions." She smiled, picturing her sister as a bright-eyed, rosy-cheeked little girl clutching a bundle of weeds. "One summer, when Mom wouldn't give her money for the ice-cream man, she decided she'd start selling them."

"Selling dandelions?"

Kayla nodded. "She gathered a bunch, tied them into bouquets and sold them door-to-door."

He threw his head back and laughed. "You're joking."

"I'm totally serious."

"Did anyone buy them?"

"I told her they wouldn't, that she was wasting her time, and suggested she find and pick lavender instead—my favorite flower." She smiled. "But she proved me wrong. Seemed no one could turn down a cute little girl with big brown eyes and pigtails." Kayla picked up a twig near her shoe and broke it into pieces.

"Lavender, huh? I would've pegged you as a carnation girl."

"When I see all this—" she motioned toward the open door "—that's the Christy I remember." The Christy she wanted back.

She was determined to do whatever she could to see that happen. The first step was to get this place clean, and find and toss out every ounce of alcohol and whatever other garbage Christy had stored here.

She stood and dusted the dirt off her hands. "I should probably get busy."

"Doing what?"

"Cleaning. I know it probably seems pointless, but seeing all this… I feel I have to do something, you know?"

He studied her for a long moment, then said, "I've got some time. I'll help."

Kayla smiled as they went inside, warmth pushing out the chill that sorrow for her sister had created.

Maybe she and Noah could work together after all.

For the good of the children.

Nothing more.

She grabbed a garbage bag and snapped it open. "You wanted to talk to me about something?"

He tossed an empty liquor bottle into the bag. "Yeah. You don't happen to have any clients in need of rustic furniture, do you?"

"Like what your ministry makes?"

He nodded.

She tossed three more bottles into the trash. She wasn't sure what John Kollings might want for his law firms, but he'd likely lean toward modern-chic. Still, she could ask. "How many pieces were you hoping to place?"

"As many as I can." He gave a sheepish laugh. "We're being sued. The lawsuit is completely without merit, but we'll still need to hire a lawyer."

"That's expensive."

"Exactly. And we're bare-bonesing it as it is."

She glanced around, cleared off a section of the couch, sat and motioned for Noah to join her. "Can you tell me more about your ministry? I mean, I know you help drug addicts and alcoholics."

He nodded. "Anyone seventeen and older who is self-destructing, really. Men who are homeless, near homeless, or fresh out of jail or prison. Some of them are directed to us by their parole officers. Others come on their own. The latter tend to be more successful."

"So they come make furniture?"

"That's part of it. That's how they earn a wage. But they have to stay active in our program. Counseling, group therapy, Bible studies, life-skill classes. Some go through an anger-management course. We create a unique personal-growth plan for each man, then monitor his progress."

Anger management? Hearing that only heightened her concerns regarding the ministry and her niece and nephew spending time in such an environment. But all that aside, she had to admit, Noah had created an impressive arrangement. She'd love to see Christy get involved with something like that. But she knew she'd never go willingly.

She'd need a parole officer or someone similar to force her growth.

"What do you think?" Noah rubbed his fist in his palm.

"I don't know if any of my current clients are shopping for rustic furniture, but I can make some calls." She pulled up her calendar on her phone. "Tell you what. Send me what you've got along with prices, including any bulk discounts." That was how she'd gotten started, making cold calls. No reason she couldn't do it again. Maybe a Skagit Valley hotel or wedding venue would be interested in some refurbishing.

"I really appreciate it."

His boyish smile, so full of hope, tugged on her heart in a way she refused to process.

Chapter Five

Noah's mare, a twenty-three-year-old mixed palomino, neighed a greeting the moment his boots hit the stable breezeway. Soon, the others started to whicker and poke their heads over their stall gates.

"All right, y'all. I hear you." He paused at the large barrel outside the coachman's room to scoop grain into a bucket. This triggered snorting and more nickering.

He grabbed a handful of grain and approached his mare, Velvet. "How you holding up, ol' girl?" She'd been his first horse, hard-earned through lots of stall mucking and sweat. The rodeo bug hit him not long after, first with tie-down roping, then saddle-bronc riding. Rode his first bull a year and a half later.

Boots clicked on the cement, and he turned to see Elliot approach carrying a flat-bottomed shovel. His jeans looked two sizes too big, and sweat stains darkened his T-shirt.

Noah brushed grain crumbs from his hand. "What're you doing here?"

"Figured you could use my help." Elliot Jordan had the build and endurance of a forty-year-old despite being in his midsixties, a fact Noah was grateful for.

"Stall mucking isn't exactly in your job description."

"It is when the boss man lands in a tornado."

Every man needed a friend and ministry partner like Elliot. "Not sure it's that bad." Though it all was wearing on him—the ministry, caring for the kids, worrying about his parents, dealing with conflicting emotions regarding Kayla.

Elliot raised an eyebrow. "Those dark circles under your eyes tell a different story."

"Oh, I'm tired, for sure."

"How long you think you can keep this up, running the kids to your parents, bringing them to the ministry? You need a nanny, bro." He clapped a hand on Noah's shoulder.

"The good ones cost more than I can afford." Plus, he wasn't sure how the kids would deal with having one more new person in their lives.

Elliot leaned a shoulder against the outer stall wall and crossed his arms. "How'd things go with Kayla and your parents? Did she throw a fit?"

"No, but she's pretty shook up. Processing where her sister's at, probably coming to terms with the fact that Christy's not likely to kick her addictions. Least, not anytime soon." He told him about all their cleaning the previous afternoon.

"Seems to me you've been there."

"You talking about JD?" Noah hadn't seen his brother in over six months. The guy hadn't even bothered to show up for the birth of his little girl. "If only I hadn't brought him to the Longhorn Bronc and Steer."

"Oh, I see. Because he caught the bull-riding bug and bucked common sense to the manure pile, you're to blame for all his foolishness?"

"I should've known, bringing him to all my competitions, goading him to get up on a bull…" But back then,

Noah had been making good money, winning national titles. He'd fully anticipated a long, successful career and wanted his brother to have the same—with little thought of all the broken bones that came with it. But then again, that'd been part of the allure. He'd felt strong, invincible, something his wounded, beaten-down heart had needed after years of feeling weak and helpless as a kid. JD probably felt the same.

It'd taken the loss of a friend and a coma that nearly broke his mama to finally pull Noah out of bull-riding. Hopefully, JD would have some sense knocked into him, literally or figuratively, much sooner.

"You couldn't have known your brother would lose his brains in a tequila bottle."

Noah gave a slight shrug. "And take Christy Fisher along with him."

"No one forced her. That girl followed your brother down the addiction trail all on her own."

"I get what you're saying."

"But you're still carrying guilt."

He massaged his temple. "Watching my niece and nephew suffer as a result of all this? Yeah."

"So now what?"

"I don't know. All's I can do is love on Timber and Sophia best as I can."

"And Kayla?"

Heat crept up his neck. "What about her?"

"You going to let her help with the kids? Because everything you're feeling right now, she's bearing it, too. Only more so, because she's looking in from the outside."

"We might be working together soon enough." He told Elliot about their furniture discussion.

"That's great, but that doesn't give her a voice as far as the kids are concerned."

"She's trying to get approved by the state to watch the kids." He explained the process. "I'll follow up with her to see if she's heard back."

"I'm sure she'd appreciate that."

Though truth be told, Noah wasn't sure he wanted her to have a voice, least not if it meant taking the kids. But surely she wouldn't do anything to uproot those children further. She had to see how connected they were here in Sage Creek, the way the community had rallied around them.

And if Christy returned? How would that affect them? What if they needed to move out of the Hill Country, somewhere where they could have a fresh start?

He wasn't ready to consider that, might never be. But Elliot was probably right about letting Kayla become more involved. Those kids were her kin, too, and he needed to start allowing them into her care. "I'll call her."

Elliot grinned. "Good man." Whistling, he grabbed his shovel and headed into River's stall while Noah phoned Kayla.

"Noah, hi. I've been putting out a few fires and haven't had a chance to make any calls yet. Sorry."

"That's not why I'm contacting you."

"Oh? Is everything all right with Timber and Sophia?"

"Huh? They're doing great. I wasn't calling about them. I mean, I was, but not because anything's wrong. What I want to say is, would you like to come to supper tonight? At my parents' place?" Twice in less than a week. Three times and this might become a habit, not that he was opposed to the idea. Though common sense said he should be, considering the way his pulse quickened every time he heard her voice or saw that sweet smile of hers.

Silence.

Elliot's shovel scraped against cement.

"If you don't wa—"

"No," she said. "Supper would be good. What time?"

"Ah…" He should probably call his folks. Make sure they had plenty of brisket to spare, though he couldn't imagine Kayla would eat much. She weighed a buck and change, max. "Six thirty?" That'd give him time to grab a shower and swing by the grocery, if need be.

"That works. Thanks."

He hung up, unable to suppress a silly grin.

This was bad. His reaction to her coming to dinner…

She was stirring emotions in him he had no business allowing, especially considering, by month's end, she'd likely be heading back to Washington State.

And potentially taking Timber and Sophia with her.

Maybe if he remembered that—what all was at stake here—he'd quit acting like a girl-crazy schoolboy.

Attempting to avert his thoughts, he checked his emails on the way to his truck. Most were spam, but one from Pastor Roger listed foster-care training classes, all at least an hour away. Another was a response to a message he'd sent to a men's ministry leader two towns over inviting him to come in for a meeting.

Something he for sure needed to do, if he wanted to drum up the funding his ministry needed to stay afloat. But first, he and his board needed to figure out how they were going to handle the lawsuit. *Lord, any chance You'll just make that go away?* If only he had more time.

Even with his parents' help, this single-parenting thing was hard.

How willing was Kayla to help? Bigger question—how much could he trust her to do? Hopefully tonight would provide answers to that question.

He stepped into his truck, the scent of sour milk reminding him to steam-clean the interior. He needed to make sure the lid of Timber's sippy cup was screwed on tightly.

Half a dozen or so country songs later, he arrived at his parents' house anxious to roughhouse with his giggly nephew and smell Sophia's sweet baby scent. He could use some of the peace his mom always managed to dish out, too.

Hopefully, Kayla's joining them for dinner wouldn't sabotage any of that.

A brisk breeze that seemed to threaten rain swept over him as he stepped out of his truck and strode up his parents' walk. The rusted screen hinges whined as he pushed his way inside.

He hung his Stetson on a hook near the door and scanned the dim and silent living room. "Hey-lo?"

"I'm in here."

He followed the sound of his mother's voice into the kitchen. "Where're the little ones?" The scent of baking bread rolls wafted from the oven and…he took another sniff. "Is that peach cobbler I smell?"

His mom smiled and greeted him with a kiss to the cheek. "Yep, and Timber and Sophia are napping. They have been going on three hours now."

He raised an eyebrow. "Sounds like Nana plumb wore them out."

"Maybe just a little." Her smile radiated pure joy. Grandparenting looked good on her, and with how she was grieving his father's mental decline, she could use every drop of sunshine the good Lord sent her way.

"Nice day at work?"

"Not bad." He grabbed a knife. "Need me to slice the tomatoes and cucumbers?"

His mom stirred gravy in a steaming pan and nodded.

"Thank you." She shared a funny story from her book club, then asked if he'd heard from Kayla.

"Nothing regarding potential furniture sales. But I did speak to her this afternoon. Shortly before heading here."

"Oh? How's she holding up? It has to be painful, to learn about her sister's behavior, not to mention dealing with her disappearance."

Mom would know with all the tears she'd cried for both him and his brother—the tears she still shed for JD, most likely.

He placed a ripe tomato, likely fresh out of his mom's garden, onto a cutting block. "I invited her for dinner."

His mom halted in midstir, then resumed. "When?"

"Tonight."

He waited for her response, finished slicing the tomato then moved on to the cucumber.

"You're upset," he said.

"Concerned. She seemed pretty guarded, and watchful, last time she was here. Like she was doing all she could to rein in her words. Almost like she was thinking of snatching those precious grandchildren of mine and making a dash for it."

"I'd outrun her easy." His joke failed to make her laugh.

"What if she decides to make trouble?"

"I've talked with her, Mom. She wants what's best for the kids."

"I'm sure that's true, but does she believe what's best is them here? With us?"

The doorbell rang, and his mom turned back to her gravy. "Can you get that? I need a minute. To pray."

He nodded. With a sigh, he exited the kitchen and crossed through the small living room. Maybe he shouldn't have invited Kayla? Or at least, he should've given his mom more warning.

Too late for coulda-shouldas now. He took a deep breath and opened the door.

"Hi." Kayla's shy smile captivated him. Wearing a scoop-necked blouse that brought out the blush in her skin, and with her hair wind-tousled, her beauty left him temporarily speechless.

Tiny lines formed on her delicate brow. "Am I early?" She held a bakery container that looked like it was from Wilma's.

"No—no." His brain and tongue finally caught up with his galloping pulse. He stepped aside. "Come in."

She did, carrying with her the soft scents of strawberry and jasmine. "I brought dessert." She handed over the item, then inhaled and frowned. "Your mom already made something, didn't she?"

He eyed the box—the sticker on top indicated it was a sweet-potato spice cake. "You can never have too many baked goods, right?"

"I guess." She looked unconvinced. Poor girl probably felt even more awkward than he did. Yet she was here. Strong woman. He admired her gumption.

"Kayla, so good to see you." His mom emerged from the kitchen untying her apron, which she deposited on the back of the couch. She gave Kayla a somewhat stiff hug.

"Thank you for inviting me." Kayla clutched one hand in the other and glanced around. "Where are the—"

Fussing sounded from the baby monitor on the counter. "I'll get the little munchkins." Mom dashed out, almost as if she expected Kayla to fight her for wake-up duty.

Noah and Kayla stood there, staring at one another. Why had all cohesive thoughts, and the intelligent conversation he hoped they'd spur, suddenly vacated his brain?

* * *

Kayla suppressed a smile as she listened to Noah fumble with his words. All big and strong and rough-and-tumble cowboy on the outside, but tender and almost boyish underneath.

"Y'all ready to eat?" Noah's mother stood in the kitchen entryway, swaying a contented Sophia in her arms while a rosy-cheeked Timber peeked around her skirt. "Because little man here is hungry." She mussed his hair. "Apparently all the food he put away this afternoon went straight through him. That boy must be about to have a growth spurt."

Noah's brow furrowed. "Didn't we just buy him new clothes?"

"That we did." She kissed the top of Sophia's head. "Little ones have a funny way of growing on us."

He laughed.

Kayla stepped closer and stroked the child's cheek with the back of her hand. "Hey there, princess."

His mother dropped her gaze momentarily, then straightened and met Kayla's eye. "Want to hold her?"

Kayla smiled. "I'd love to. Thank you."

Mrs. Williams handed over Sophia. Cradling the child in her arms, Kayla followed Noah's lead to a chair he'd pulled away from the table. She watched Timber tiptoe over cracks in the tiles. When he looked her way, she said, "How's the big boy doing? Did you help mind the baby?"

Timber's chubby-cheeked smile nearly swallowed his eyes. He nodded, grabbed Sophia's pacifier off the floor—it must have fallen—and darted to her side.

"Binky." He held it out for her.

Such an adorable little guy! "Why, thank you, Timber." She wrapped her arm around his waist and gave a squeeze. "That was very thoughtful of you."

"Oh, he shares real good, don't you, budster?" Noah winked at his nephew.

"I think you call him something different each time." His mom placed a pitcher of ice water on the table. "You must have a storehouse of nicknames somewhere."

"Yep. Right here." He grinned and tapped his temple.

Seeing his paternal side, how gentle and engaged he was with the children, drew Kayla to him.

His mom shook her head. "What'm I going to do with you, boy?"

"Just feed me, and I'll be happy."

"Oh, I know that's right." She glanced toward the living room. "Y'all have a seat. I'll go fetch your father."

Once she'd returned with her husband in tow, Noah plucked Timber up beneath his armpit and positioned him into his high chair. Then Noah returned for Sophia. "Time for your swing, little miss, so your aunt Kayla can eat something."

Kayla relinquished her sweet bundle and scooted closer to the kitchen table, which Noah's mom had covered with food.

"So, Kayla…" Mrs. Williams sat beside her husband and began scooping food onto his plate. He didn't seem interested. "Noah tells me you're an interior designer now?"

"Yes, ma'am. In northern Washington. My business is primarily in Bellingham, but I have clients throughout the Puget Sound area."

"Such a beautiful place." She sliced into her potato. "How'd you get into that?"

"Almost by accident." She laughed. "I started helping my friends decorate their houses, as wedding gifts. Pretty soon, their friends started asking if I'd help them with their homes, and before I knew it, I had a sizable client list." Three years later, she'd moved to real-estate staging and then, eventually, into the high-dollar market of Whidbey Island and West Seattle.

Mrs. Williams squirted some barbecue sauce first on her plate, then on her husband's. "How long do you plan on staying in Sage Creek?"

Kayla watched Timber dunk a potato wedge in ketchup. "I'm not exactly sure how to answer that question. I just learned all the options today."

Noah's fork stopped midway to his mouth. "Options?"

She nodded. "I finally heard back from Timber and Sophia's case worker. She asked a lot of questions regarding where I live and my relationship with the children."

"And what did you tell them?" Mrs. Williams's voice sounded pinched.

"That I love them and wanted the best for them."

"But that you haven't been around much?"

Kayla flinched inwardly as a familiar wave of guilt swept over her. "I acknowledged the frequency of my visits."

"*In*frequency," Mrs. Williams said.

"Excuse me?"

"Infrequency. You acknowledged the infrequency?"

"Mom." Noah placed a hand on her forearm.

A stretch of silence, other than the sounds of utensils against plates and Sophia's frequent babble, followed.

"It's been fun watching Timber in the nursery." Mrs. Williams kept her gaze on her plate. "He's making friends and seems to be connecting with the volunteers. Kayla, you should come watch him sometime. It's precious to see."

Kayla nodded. She couldn't help but feel Mrs. Williams's statement held an ulterior motive.

"Did Noah tell you we plan to register the little man for

preschool this spring?" Mrs. Williams cast her son a side-ways glance. "That way he'll be able to catch up socially."

In other words, her sister had kept him isolated and thus developmentally delayed. Was that Mrs. Williams's implication? The even bigger question seemed to be, was that true?

Timber's high chair squeaked as he bounced and kicked his legs. Deeply engaged in finger-painting his tray with ketchup, he chattered and chirped with a myriad of random, nonsensical sounds.

After a few more minutes of awkward silence, Noah's stepdad pushed away from the table, leaving over half of his plate untouched.

Mrs. Williams stood and placed a hand on his shoulder. "Sit, dear, and finish your supper."

Backing away, he shook his head.

"Would you like some ice cream?" She moved toward the freezer, and Mr. Williams inched back to the table.

"Ice cweam!" Timber slammed a ketchup-covered fist onto his high-chair tray. "Me some! Me some!"

"Not until you finish your veggies." Noah pointed to Timber's plate.

The child poked out his bottom lip and started to cry. "Ice cweam, Nana. Pwease."

She sighed. "Sorry, Noah, but there's no way I can say no to that sweet face."

He rolled his eyes. "You're going to spoil him something awful."

She pulled some bowls from the cupboard. "That's what nanas are for." But then her gaze shot to Kayla, and her face sobered. "The boy's eaten well today. Grapes, half a banana, fish sticks for lunch. Figure he deserves some dessert every now and then." She brought two bowls, one filled with a small amount, the other holding about as much as it could, back to the table. "It's about all he'll eat anymore." She placed the larger serving in front of her husband.

Soon, the youngest and oldest males at the table were happily eating their unexpected treats.

Mrs. Williams sat back down and returned her napkin to her lap. "How are your parents, dear?"

"My grandparents?" When Kayla received a quizzical look, she added, "My parents died in a plane crash when I was thirteen."

"Oh. I'm so sorry. That must've been so very hard."

It had been, for her sister most of all. She'd turned surly after that, and defiant. Like she had to test every boundary, not to mention their grandparents' last drop of patience. They always responded with love, no matter what she did or said, or how many fits she threw. Some accused them of being overly lenient.

Maybe those people had been right.

It was time they talked about the reason she'd come. She took a sip of water. "They'd love to see the children. Perhaps for a weekend."

Forks clanked against plates as Noah and his mom took a sudden interest in their food. Were they afraid her grandparents might want custody of the kids? Would they? Would they even have the energy to chase after a toddler? With her help, maybe. But she couldn't stay in Texas long-term, not without neglecting her business. "They recognize there are hoops they need to jump through. That they'll likely need to get okayed by the social worker Emma Jenson."

Noah pushed away his now empty plate. "For now, seems this here is the best situation." He motioned to include everyone sitting around the table. "Gives you time to get to know the kids better without them getting jostled around too much."

That was a clear claim of territory if she'd ever heard one.

"That said, while you're here, I figure we should all be figuring out ways to work together."

Mrs. Williams dabbed her mouth with her napkin and stood. "Cobbler, anyone?"

In other words, Kayla could see the kids on *their* turf and *their* terms. Not that she blamed them, really. They'd obviously spent a lot of time with the children and had grown quite attached. And it was clear they loved them, but with Noah's ministry and his dad's mental condition—though she couldn't be certain, she'd say he suffered from Alzheimer's or dementia—this situation might not be the best.

The problem was, she wasn't certain hers would be any better, except for the fact that none of her neighbors had rap sheets.

That she knew of.

"We're not trying to shut you out." Noah touched her forearm, his hand warm and strong against her skin. "I promise."

She wanted to believe him, and sitting there, staring into his gentle eyes, she almost did. Almost forgot her entire reason for coming to Sage Creek in the first place.

Which she couldn't let happen. Somehow she had to figure out a way to partner with this man, for Timber and Sophia's sake, without getting caught up in any messy feelings.

Chapter Six

The next morning, Noah met one of Pastor Roger's old seminary friends for lunch. Apparently, the guy had numerous connections. Very generous connections.

"After you." He held the door of Wilma's Café open for Mr. Brown. "You ever had one of Wilma's famous char-grilled, Wagyu-beef burgers?" Stepping in behind the man, Noah scanned the dining area. His gaze landed on Kayla, looking so studious and beautiful, sitting hunched over a laptop and a bunch of documents. Dressed in a powder blue blouse and black slacks, she alternated between chewing the end of her pen and staring at the screen in front of her.

"Do we seat ourselves?"

Noah's face heated at Mr. Brown's question and the realization that he'd been standing there, staring at Kayla, for much too long. Especially considering he was here to make a good impression on the man.

He gave a slight cough. "How about over there?" He motioned to an empty booth near the back.

Sally Jo, the owner's daughter, passed by with a pitcher of sweet tea in one hand and a steaming coffeepot in the other. "Good afternoon, fellas. I'll be with you in a bit."

Noah nodded and led the way to his favorite table, tipping his hat at Kayla en route. Her eyes widened, and the most adorable blush colored her cheeks. She offered a nod and slight smile, which was tinged with a hint of sorrow, or perhaps caution, before she returned to her work.

"So I should order the burger, huh?" Mr. Brown's question once again jolted Noah back to the present.

Noah smiled. "Best burger east of the Great Divide."

"You've sold me."

They ordered and sipped the sweet tea Sally Jo brought them while they waited for their food.

"Pastor Roger says you've got quite a thing going at that ministry of yours." Mr. Brown slid aside his place setting and folded his hands on the table. "Tell me more about it."

"What would you like to know?"

"Why'd you launch the ministry in the first place?"

"I was a problem teenager. Started going to parties—wherever I could find liquor, really—midway through my freshman year of high school. Got into bull-riding pretty young, and didn't do too bad for myself. I traveled the country competing in one rodeo after another."

"I've heard that can be addicting."

He nodded. "I loved the rush."

Sally deposited their food with a smile.

Mr. Brown picked up his fork. "And the ladies?"

Noah chuckled. "That was a perk, for sure." Like with any sport, bull riders had their share of groupies—women who followed cowboys around, batting their eyes and acting all cute.

"So why'd you quit? You get hurt?"

"Plenty of times, but not even a set of broken ribs could keep me down for long. But then I lost one of my friends. He flew off a bull and snapped his neck. At first, that only drove me to the bottle and the next competition. But then, not even a week later, I landed myself into a coma. I woke to find my mama sitting at my bedside looking so…broken."

"How long had you been out?"

"Long enough for my mom to think she'd lost me. I know she'd worried about that before. I can't imagine the nights she spent up, praying for my safety, wondering if I'd return home paralyzed or worse. Never really bothered me before, least not enough to change me. But this time was different, because I knew what it felt like to lose someone you love."

"Your friend?"

Noah nodded. "I realized I couldn't do that to my mama anymore."

"So where does your ministry fit in?"

"After that accident, I moved in with my mom and stepdad, and he immediately put me to work making furniture. Said I needed to earn my keep. At first I was pretty ticked about the whole deal. I'd been making bank riding bulls, and here I was, working for a steak sandwich and a place to crash. But then I saw the results of all my labor. First thing I made was a jewelry box for my mama."

The pride he'd felt, sanding down the edges, carving out intricate flowers and vines. And seeing her face when he gave it to her. She'd been even more touched than he'd envisioned. "When I gave it to her, she hardly could get a word out. Just started crying and hugging me and crying some more."

"Because you'd made something just for her."

"That, and I think she understood what was going on inside me even more than I did. In helping me create something beautiful, my stepdad was breathing life and hope into my soul. And that's what I want to do for the men we serve. I want to see the life in them and call it out."

"Impressive. And y'all sell what your guys make to fund the ministry?"

"In theory." He took a swig of his drink. "Problem is, seventy percent of our guys are in training." That alone, lawsuit not included, would've been enough to spike his blood pressure. If they didn't figure out a way to bring in some major income soon, the ministry wouldn't survive.

"Which means inventory is low."

"Lower than we'd like." Their work was too important to let the place tank.

"And that's where Team Missions comes in, correct?"

"We would like your organization to partner with us as donors, yes."

While Noah shared his organization's vision and philosophy, he tried to remain focused on the conversation, but his thoughts kept drifting to Kayla. The way she laughed whenever Timber mispronounced something or zoomed about the room. The loving way she gazed down on Sophia, whenever she cradled the infant in her arms. And now the inner strength and determination her features displayed, as she worked through whatever documents she'd laid before her.

She was hardworking, compassionate, traits any man would want in a woman.

Not that he was looking. Though he might want to consider finding a wife eventually, for the kids' sake, seeing how he was raising them and all.

"Well…" Mr. Brown crumpled his napkin and tossed it on his nearly cleaned plate. "You've given me a good deal to think about." He pulled out his wallet and dropped two twenties on the table.

"This one's on me." Noah tried to give them back.

Chapter Seven

"So Kayla's approved to watch the kids on her own?" Noah leaned against the wall, one hand crossed over his chest, as Emma Jenson, Timber and Sophia's social worker, shared her conversation with Kayla.

"Yes, she is."

"Timber might act up some."

"He'll be all right," she said. "It'll be good for the both of them. Give them time to bond."

"I'll let her know."

"I've already spoken with her."

"Okay, thanks, Emma. I'll talk to her tonight to get things set up." He was looking forward to the extra help where the kids were concerned, but worried about where her involvement might lead. "Thanks for keeping me in the loop." He ended the call, grabbed the pages he'd printed off from his desk and walked to the bedroom-turned-conference-room.

The rest of his team were already there and waiting for him. "Sorry I'm late." He distributed Helping Hands' financials, then sat. A thick silence filled the room as everyone read through the numbers.

Joe, an advisory-board member, spoke first. "Now

that we know where the ministry stands, we can figure out a solution."

The board secretary tapped a pencil in her palm. "Where are we at with the lawsuit?"

Terrance pulled a manila file from his briefcase. "I met with five law firms, one from Sage Creek, another from Rockdale, two from Austin and one from Houston. I know this might be a bit inconvenient, but I suggest we go with the Houston lawyer. Sound good to you, Noah?"

Driving back and forth would take a chunk of time out of his already tight schedule, but he agreed with Joe. "Makes sense. What's our next step?"

"I'll set up an appointment for later this week. Not sure how much flexibility we'll have with that. Brenda, think you can clear Noah's schedule to accommodate?"

"I'll have to, won't I?"

"How much does he want for a retainer?" Noah asked.

Terrance distributed a sheet of paper with the lawyer's fees.

"Any chance the guy will work pro bono?" Elliot asked.

Terrance shook his head. "Believe me, I tried."

"All right." Elliot leaned back and crossed his arms. "So what's the plan to pay the retainer?"

Noah relayed his conversation with Kayla. "Only problem is, there's no telling if any of those Seattle companies will take our stuff, and when we'll receive payment once they do."

Joe riffled through the papers in front of him and placed their financials on top. "We've got to pay this, regardless." Reading the numbers, he pulled on the skin of his throat. "I'll send the guy a check first thing tomorrow."

"And what happens when we don't have money for rent?" Elliot asked.

Joe gave a one-shoulder shrug. "We pray God comes through."

Elliot's frown deepened. "And if He doesn't?"

"Look, I understand your concern." Noah didn't like taking such a big risk with ministry funds any more than Elliot did. "But either way, we lose. If we don't address this lawsuit, it'll cost us a whole lot more than a month's rent." He paused. "Anyone try calling up our past donors or holiday-only givers?"

"Yeah." Terrance sighed. "Seems everyone's tight. Giving is down across the board, which also means churches have less to delegate to outside ministries. Mission organizations are struggling to keep their own people afloat."

The other board members voiced questions, ideas and concerns:

"Maybe we could drum up some kind of social-media campaign."

"What if we partnered with one of them?"

"I thought that's what we've been trying to do. To form ongoing partnerships."

"No, what I mean is, what if we came under one of their umbrellas?"

Noah rubbed the back of his neck. Truth was, he'd thought of that numerous times, but was worried how that'd play out long-term. "We'd lose our autonomy, and with it, potentially our decision-making power."

Heads nodded.

"But God's bigger, right?" Joe smiled. "Meaning, so long as we're leaning on Him and following His lead, we can trust His purposes will prevail—for our ministry, those we serve and all those in similar places of brokenness and defeat."

Noah glanced at his phone. He needed to pick up Kayla soon. Warmth spread through him as an image of her sweet smile came to mind. That woman was beautiful, inside and out. And completely off-limits, romantically speaking. Somehow his rebellious heart kept forgetting that fact. "On that note, how about we adjourn for the evening and commit this, and all of our concerns and uncertainties, to prayer?"

Everyone agreed, so Joe closed the meeting with a confident yet beseeching request for God's guidance and the peace to wait until He chose to reveal the next steps.

Those were two things Noah longed to experience in his own life, as well. He knew intellectually that God had a perfect plan, for his ministry, his parents, the kids, him and Kayla. But that didn't mean Noah's desires and God's will would coincide. What if God wanted to move those kids out of Texas, way out to Washington, with Kayla?

He wasn't sure what stung more—the thought of losing the children who had become such a huge and precious part of his life, or the woman who'd awakened his desire for a family, something he'd long since written off.

To love a woman deeply and experience her love in return.

Noah excused himself with a tip of his Stetson. "Hate to skedaddle just when y'all are getting to the fun business." He indicated the nearly untouched tray of cookies and brownies his board members were just beginning to devour.

They laughed and waved him off.

Leaving his team to gab over the plethora of baked goods Brenda had brought, he grabbed his jacket and hustled to his truck. Using his Bluetooth, he contacted Lucy Carr, an older lady from the church, to check on the kids—she'd volunteered to watch them overnight so he could go to his board meeting, then to the foster class after. He didn't know what he'd do without her and the other ladies from Trinity Faith Church. Though his mama tried, she simply couldn't be there for the kids like she wanted. But thanks to his church family, he and the kids had all the support they needed.

He called Kayla next. "I'm heading your way. Just leaving work now."

"I'm at the Literary Sweet Spot catching up on emails and such," Kayla said. "Mind picking me up here?"

"Perfect. So, um, the kids' social worker called."

"And?"

"When did you want to start spending time with the kids, and what might that look like?"

She paused. "I've got video conferences nearly back-to-back tomorrow, but I could be at your place first thing the day after. Were you hoping I'd nanny full-time?"

"I suspect that'll be difficult for you, managing your design business and all."

"A little. But I'll do whatever you need."

He had no doubt she would, even if it cost her part of her livelihood, and he admired her for that. "I take most Friday mornings off, and usually spend the afternoons running errands. The quilting ladies from church usually have stuff planned for the kids on Mondays. They're always looking for additional ragamuffins to grandparent."

He mentally reviewed his calendar. "I suspect Mom will probably want them once a week, too. When she's able to take them." A lot of that depended on how things went with his dad. Some days, she was plumb frazzled, others she needed the dash of sunshine those kiddos brought. Noah was willing to stay flexible, rearrange his schedule if need be, to allow that.

"Which leaves three days a week. From what, eight to five?"

"Give or take."

She released what sounded like a relieved sigh. "I can do that."

"Timber might fuss a bit in the beginning—he did for me when I first started minding him. But just take him out to feed carrots to the horses, and he'll cheer up right quick."

"You have horses?"

"They're out back in the stable. Three of 'em. Two that are older than mud and a third that's got too much life in her, if you ask my mama."

"Feisty, huh?"

"Oh, she's something. Probably pawing at the ground ready to break free of her stall as we speak. If Elliot— he's on staff at Helping Hands—hasn't let them out to pasture already. If you go, make sure to bring some carrots. Give one or two to Timber, so he can feed them. He thinks that's the funniest thing since little Sophia got a bout of the hiccups."

"I bet that was hilarious."

"The little man will keep you entertained, that's for sure."

"I'm looking forward to it."

So was he—looking forward to seeing Kayla, that was. And that worried him.

He spent the rest of the drive praying—for wisdom with regard to his ministry, for the energy and perseverance to keep moving forward as he tried to juggle it all. For God's intervention regarding the lawsuit and that He would keep those kids in Sage Creek, where they belonged.

He arrived at the Literary Sweet Spot to find Kayla sitting outside.

She glanced up as he approached, and a beautiful smile lit her eyes, nearly stealing his breath.

"Howdy." He tipped his hat at her, feeling similar to how he did before taking Judy Blaese, his first-ever crush, to the sixth-grade bowling party. Hopefully this little jaunt to Houston wouldn't be nearly as awkward.

"Hey." Her cheeks colored as she quickly gathered her things, which appeared to be a bunch of notes and home decor catalogs and magazines, then stood.

"Hard at work, I see." He led the way to his truck, then held the passenger-side door open for her. A breeze swept her familiar jasmine-strawberry scent toward him, halting his brain.

"Something like that. I heard back from two of the Seattle stores we discussed."

"Yeah?" Hope pricked.

"They expressed definite interest. When can you, Faith and I meet to go over your promotional material?"

"She said she'd get back to me later this week." Seemed maybe God was already starting to answer his prayers. *Lord, keep it up, please. Because we've got a long ways to go yet.*

"Perfect."

A honk from a car passing behind him helped jolt his thoughts back to coherency. With a slap to the roof of his cab, he grinned, closed her door, rounded the truck, then slid in behind the steering wheel.

He started the engine, and a rush of cool air flooded out of the vents. The chorus of an old country-western song that triggered memories from his bull-riding days played through the speakers.

Kayla gazed out her side window as the town's storefronts gave way to pastureland dotted by the occasional farmhouse. "The church still hold its annual picnic each summer?"

"Yep. Going on…might be fifty years or more now."

"You going?"

"Wouldn't miss it for anything. I plan to enter Timber in the big wheels race."

"The what?"

"They might have added that activity on after you left. To give the little ones something to do. A bunch of us set up a makeshift race track in the park, corral all the kids aged two to four on sets of big wheels and watch them go."

She laughed. "I bet it's adorable."

"It is at that. You should come."

"If I'm still here, I will."

His heart pinched at the reminder that she didn't plan to stay long.

She pulled a tube of fruity-smelling lotion from her purse and rubbed it into her hands. "It's nice to know some things don't change."

"The picnic, you mean?"

"That and so many other Sage Creek traditions, but most importantly, the fact that everyone pulls together. I can't help but wonder how things might've played out differently, for Timber and Sophia, if Christy had been more connected in the community. Had let folks help her out more."

He'd asked the same question, numerous times. Not just regarding Christy, but nearly every addict who came through his ministry's doors. They all had stories, often generations' worth. But one thing most of them didn't have was deep faith ties. God told His children to care for one another, and the folks at church sure were doing their best, but there wasn't much they could do with unwilling recipients.

He laid a hand on her forearm. "I'm sorry this is so hard. I get it. I really do."

She studied him as if gauging the reliability of his words, then gave a quick nod. "I know you do. Your brother, do you have any idea where he is now?"

"Nope. He never contacts me unless he wants money or has landed in some sort of trouble. And he for sure wouldn't tell me where to find him, for fear I'd come drag him back home and into rehab."

"Do you think he knows? About the kids, I mean?"

"Last I heard, their social worker hadn't been able to track him down, which doesn't surprise me. He's probably still out chasing after the next rodeo, crashing at cheap motels whenever and wherever he can."

"Like you used to do?"

He nodded, thinking back to those chaotic days. "I rode my first bull in high school. Lasted maybe three seconds and thought for sure I'd ripped my arm clean out of my socket."

"Ouch."

He chuckled. "Found out not long after what a true dislocated shoulder feels like. And broken ribs, busted jaw, cracked skull…"

"Seriously? You experienced all that?"

He nodded.

"Why didn't you stop?"

"Lots of reasons. Bull-riding made me feel strong. Powerful. Plus, it pays good. The best of the best can make up to two hundred thousand annually."

"And the not-so-best?"

"A lot less."

"Which were you?"

"Somewhere in between. Though I never earned enough to make folks jealous, I didn't do too shabby for someone straight out of high school. I s'pose that was what drew me. At eighteen, nineteen, the income seemed great, but really, it was always just enough. Just enough to make my next truck payment, or buy groceries, or pay my next medical bill—so I could heal and make it to my next rodeo."

He turned onto the interstate leading to Houston. "Honestly, I chased the lifestyle more than anything else. I'm so glad God got a hold of me, otherwise I have no idea where I'd be now. Not to mention what might've happened to all the men helped by my ministry over the years."

"You must have an entrepreneur personality."

"Why do you say that?"

"To start a nonprofit. I imagine it couldn't have been easy, finding a staff, getting funding, and all that."

"Not in the least. But it started out pretty small. With me helping one guy. At the time I was meeting with Pastor Roger. Some might say he was mentoring me. I'd say it was more like he kept my sorry self in check. That man has never been afraid to speak hard truth when it needs to be said."

She laughed. "I don't know him hugely well, but I do know that about him."

"Anyway, I was growing in my faith and emotional maturity. One day, Pastor got a call from a family friend. The guy's son had fallen into addiction and was throwing his life away fast. He was constantly getting in bar fights, had been arrested a couple times, and his loved ones were afraid if something didn't change, he'd find himself in the penitentiary doing serious time. Pastor asked if I'd talk some sense into the guy."

She raised her eyebrows. "And he listened?"

Noah laughed. "Nope. Least, not until the courts ordered him to. I don't remember how it all came about, but somehow our meetings got listed as part of his parole."

"How'd the guy respond to that?"

"He was pretty angry at first, but I just told him, 'Look, you don't have to like me, but you do have to show up or get locked up. Might as well make your time useful by listening to what I have to say.' I didn't think he would, but he did. Or at least, quit running his mouth during our get-togethers. Eventually, he started to change, and if I were to guess, I'd say much thanks to all the prayers the Trinity Faith folks started tossing heavenward. Once others in the community saw how God had turned that fella's life around, they started sending others my way."

"Wow. That must have been exciting."

"Exciting, humbling, terrifying, overwhelming. I quickly discovered this whole deal was much bigger than me, so I started gathering folks around me." Like Elliot. "At first, none of us were earning a paycheck. We weren't even a nonprofit back then."

"How'd you manage financially?"

"We worked, me for my stepdad, Elliot in construction. We had a handful of other guys with us, in those early days, who've since moved on, but they all had day jobs."

"That must've been exhausting."

"It was."

"What kept you going?"

"God. That and, I suspect, in a way I was trying to save my brother through every man I helped. That and appease my guilt for how he'd ended up."

JD had gone completely off the rails by then. Only time Noah or his family heard from him was when he wanted money, and more often than not, he'd show up drunk.

He released a heavy breath. "I love that kid, you know?"

She nodded, and her eyes misted over.

He suspected she did understand, in a way no sibling ever should.

Based on the way her eyelashes fluttered, she was fighting tears. "I'm hoping someone like you, like your ministry, will reach out to my sister. And that she'll listen, like that first man you helped did to you."

Unfortunately, he'd learned a long time ago, addictions weren't that easy to kick. Recovery took a lot of gumption, a lot of support and a whole lot of Jesus. Sadly, only a few stayed clean and sober long-term. But telling Kayla that wouldn't help her heartache any.

"I know it hurts," he said. "Watching someone you love self-destruct. I wish I knew how to soften the blow. To ease your pain."

"You being here, listening. Knowing you get it. That's enough."

Chapter Eight

Kayla followed Noah down dimly lit stairs and through a narrow basement hallway to the church classroom hosting the foster-care classes. The musty air carried a chill, and goose bumps exploded on her skin. Purse draped over her shoulder, she rubbed warmth into her arms and scanned the faces seated behind rectangular tables.

She felt overdressed in her black slacks and coral blouse. Married couples, if she was guessing, occupied the room. Some young enough to be newlyweds, others with gray hair and wrinkles. A tall, swaybacked man with black hair and a full, neatly trimmed beard stood beside a desk to the left of a whiteboard.

He glanced up and smiled at Kayla and Noah. "Welcome. Have a seat wherever you'd like." He motioned toward the empty tables near the front of the room.

She nodded a greeting, and Noah tipped his hat. "Howdy." He touched her elbow, sending a jolt through her. "This look okay?" He indicated two empty seats beside a middle-aged couple.

"Sure."

He pulled out her chair, and she sat behind one of numerous thick notebooks positioned on tables. She flipped through the pages, reading the labels on each divider tab. Child abuse and neglect. Child development issues. Bonding and attachment. Supporting normalcy.

Noah whistled and sat beside her. "It's a lot, huh?"

She swallowed and nodded. Her gaze landed on one unsettling title written in bold on the page in front of her: *Helping children deal with trauma.*

Timber and Sophia hadn't been traumatized, had they?

Noah placed his hand, warm and strong, on hers. "Hey." He gave a gentle squeeze. "We'll get through this. Together."

Her heart tugged in his direction. *Together.* Her and Noah.

Except she didn't plan on staying in Sage Creek that long. She'd created a life for herself, a thriving business, in the Pacific Northwest, and his life was here.

She needed to remind herself of that every time he tossed that gentle smile her way.

The man at the front cleared his throat. "Let's get started." He spoke with a bit of a northeastern accent. "I'm Kenneth Hall, and I've been a foster-care and permanency director for just shy of fifteen years." He went on to explain his background, which included fostering over a dozen children and adopting three. "By the end of our sessions together, you'll walk away with the tools to bring hope and healing to children who've experienced trauma and abandonment."

His gaze scanned the room before briefly landing on Kayla. She shifted and focused on the notebook in front of her, feeling as if the shame of her sister's behavior fell on her.

In a way, it did. As the older sister, surely she bore some responsibility for what had happened. For not knowing, for not being around long enough and often enough to know.

"Your turn." Mr. Hall grinned at an older woman with orange-red hair and a heavily freckled complexion. "How about we go around the room, each of you sharing a bit about yourselves along with what brought you here tonight."

The woman nodded. "I'm Michelle Jockon, and this is my husband, Bill." She motioned to a balding man sitting beside her. "We have three grown children, whom we adore, empty bedrooms waiting to be filled and a whole lot of love to give to hurting children."

Though a few were here to prayerfully explore whether or not they felt called to foster care, most everyone else offered similar introductions. They were married, most with children of their own, and looking to help.

"It's just so sad." A younger woman in a navy cardigan shook her head. "To think, the adults who are supposed to love these kids most are the very ones who cause the most pain."

Then it was Kayla's turn. Her mouth felt dry as she introduced herself. "I'm here to…" She sat taller. "To learn."

Noah was next. He straightened and adjusted his Stetson. "I'm here because I've basically stepped into the Daddy role for my niece and nephew, and I need to learn to parent and everything related to that."

"You two married?" the man at the adjacent table asked.

Kayla's eyes widened. "What? No. He's my—my—"

"Friend." Noah's deep voice soothed her.

After everyone introduced themselves, they watched a movie that told the story of three different children. One, an eight-year-old with a mentally ill biological mom, had special needs. Next, a teenager shared her journey to adoption after seven years in the foster-care system. She'd been through a lot, had acted out quite a bit, but eventually found a family that held tight to her and helped her heal. In the final testimony, they heard from an eleven-year-old who'd been reunited with his birth mom.

Mr. Hall clicked off the television. "We want to do everything we can to create safe, loving, healthy environments for kids. You all can play a huge part in that."

An image arose unbidden, of her, Noah and the children sitting in a church pew. Little Sophia was sleeping in Kayla's arms and Timber was flipping through his picture Bible.

"That's all I have for tonight." Mr. Hall's voice jolted Kayla back to attention. "Any questions?"

There were a few. Then everyone gathered their things and migrated out the door.

Kayla stood on stiff legs and waited for Noah to finish a conversation with the red-haired lady.

Mr. Hall approached. "Thank you both for coming."

Kayla nodded to him as Noah joined her.

"I hope you find our classes instructive." He slipped a hand in his pocket. "But you should know, with kinship, you don't have to go through the same licensing requirements."

Noah hooked a thumb through his belt loop. "I was hoping I might learn a thing or two about corralling squirrelly two-year-olds."

"Now, that's a lofty aspiration." Mr. Hall chuckled. "You might find the kinship-support group, hosted here on Thursday evenings, beneficial."

Kayla's heart lightened. "That sounds awesome." She'd feel much more comfortable, and less ashamed, joining others who were experiencing similar situations. Those who were fighting an internal battle fueled by their love for the kids and their messed-up family members.

Noah scratched his bearded jaw. "Do you know of any similar get-togethers closer to Sage Creek?"

Mr. Hall shook his head. "Sorry."

"I'll have to think on this some. See how many nights I can head this way each week." Noah picked up his notebook.

Kayla grabbed her purse from the back of her chair and draped it over her shoulder. "I feel like I need all the help and wisdom I can get."

That would mean spending a two-hour-round-trip drive twice weekly with Noah Williams.

An idea she found much too appealing, considering she'd be heading back to Washington soon enough.

Potentially with the kids. She had a feeling he wouldn't be so friendly and charming then.

"You hungry?" Noah opened the church door for Kayla then followed her outside and into his truck.

"A little."

"I know a mean taco stand not far from here." He turned on the engine and his cab quickly filled with the twang of an acoustic guitar. He lowered the radio volume and eased onto the street.

"I'm game if you are."

He grinned as he drove through a residential area and back toward I-45. "So what'd you think?"

"Of the class, you mean?"

He nodded.

"I don't know. It was hard to see the stories of those children and hear all the things the other couples said. I guess I'm still processing it all, you know?"

"I get it."

After a couple of right turns, he parked along the curb a few blocks from Moody Park.

Kayla glanced around. "How do you know Houston so well?"

"Not sure that's the case so much as I know where to find cheap eats. Leftover skill from my rodeo days." He got out, intending to open her door for her, but she beat him to it and met him on the curb.

She hugged her torso. "You sure this area isn't sketchy?"

He followed her gaze toward a heavily shadowed auto-body shop sandwiched by a handful of other equally di-lapidated businesses with darkened windows. "Do you mean how many health violations has it racked up?" A chain-link fence bordered an empty lot across the way, and behind stood what appeared to be a grocery store.

"If that's supposed to be assuring…"

"Trust me. Is it too muggy, or buggy—" he swatted away a cluster of gnats "—for you?"

"Nah. I'd much rather the heat than the cold. Unlike you." A teasing smile lit her eyes.

"What?"

"If memory serves, you prefer a much colder climate."

He still didn't get it.

"Remember the iceberg plunge."

He laughed. How could he forget jumping into a pool stocked with ice cubes? "Anything for a good cause."

She angled her head. "Remind me, what charity was that for?"

"That, I can't tell you. All I knew was my buddies bet me a large meat-lover's pizza if I jumped into the iced pool and stayed under for five full seconds. I counted to eight just in case."

She gave him a playful shove. "You're terrible."

"Mite hard in the head, perhaps."

"Now or then?" The mischievous glint in her eye hiked his pulse.

"Hey, now." He longed to loop his hand through hers,

to tug her to his side, but didn't want to scare her off. Nor would he start something they'd never be able to finish.

Unless she stayed in Sage Creek, as unlikely as that was.

She breathed deep as they neared the taco truck—a yellow minibus-motorhome-type vehicle decorated with green, orange and blue suns and cacti. The scents of beef, garlic and cumin made his stomach rumble.

"What's good?" She studied the menu on the A-frame to their right.

"All of it."

"What do you normally get?"

"All of it."

Though she rolled her eyes, her hint of a smile indicated she found their lighthearted banter as much fun as he did. He reminded himself once again that he needed to step carefully. To keep things friendly and nothing more, focus on what was best for the children. Allowing his heart to get tangled up in a romance with their maternal aunt would only further complicate things.

They ordered, then took their food to a park bench under a nearby streetlight.

She tore off a piece of tortilla and popped it into her mouth. "Has food always been your weakness?"

He glanced at his burrito bowl, a massive concoction of meat and rice smothered in cheese and salsa, and feigned a hurt expression. "I'm not sure I like your insinuation."

She laughed, then raised an eyebrow. "All's I'm saying is, it'd take a whole lot more than pizza for me to go swimming in ice water."

"Yeah? And what's that?"

"Hmm…" She tapped her chin. "New shoes, a matching purse. Maybe tickets to the symphony. No, make that season tickets."

"You're telling me you and your friends never did anything stupid?"

"Never." She grinned. "And I'm only half joking. I was always the…obedient sister. Pretty sure my wildest adventure was when I tried out for the dance team."

He slapped a hand on his thigh. "I remember that!" He gave a low whistle. "You girls were something else, the way you'd glide across the football field."

"You remember?"

Did he ever. She'd been as beautiful then as she was now, and far too good for troublemakers like he'd been. "Hard not to. Y'all stalled up the football game every halftime."

"Ouch." Her playful shoulder nudge assured him she knew he was joking.

"Think you can teach an old blunder-foot like me some of your fancy footwork?"

Her amber eyes, peering up at him with such childlike curiosity, pulled him in. "You serious?"

Delay this evening as much as possible? Find a way to trigger her sweet laugh and create an excuse to get closer to her? "Absolutely."

"We don't have music."

"No problem." He pulled out his phone and clicked on his music app. A lively country tune came on. "Perfect."

She stood and tucked her hair behind her ears, looking as shy as a fawn tiptoeing out of the thicket for the first time. "We'll start with something simple. Old-school."

He came to her side, the strawberry scent of her shampoo invading his senses.

"Grapevine to the right, then touch." She demonstrated. "Then do the same to the left, and touch."

He copied her a few times. Then she added the next step. "Great job. Now back for three, and touch. Then forward and back, forward and scuff." She paused to watch him and grinned. "That's it. Now let's step to the beat. Ready, one, two…" And off she went, silver rays from the moon and nearby streetlight shimmering off her soft locks and accentuating her creamy complexion.

He did his best to keep up, but was soon a laughing, stumbling mess of feet.

"So?" He adjusted his hat. "What do you think? Am I ready for the big time yet?"

"Keep practicing and you might be able to snag a spot on the tiny-tots dance team."

"Is that right?" He pulled her closer and led her in a two-step, one of her hands smooth and soft in his, the other one light on his shoulder. Common sense told him to stop and distance himself from her, but his heart urged him to keep her close. "And how about now?"

"When did you—"

He spun her around, and when a slower song came on, he transitioned them to a country-nightclub two-step. She felt so right in his arms, followed his lead so easily, was completely relaxed.

Her gaze latched on to his, intensified.

There was no hint of the tension or distrust she'd carried into his ministry that day she'd first tumbled into Sage Creek.

A passing driver blared his horn, and she startled and pulled away, glanced at the street then back at him. She took half a step backward, increasing the distance between them. "It's getting late, and I have a conference call in the morning."

"Right."

Smart girl. One of them needed to keep their heads about them, because he surely didn't seem able to.

Not when Kayla Fisher was around, anyway.

Chapter Nine

That night, Kayla tossed and turned, catching maybe five hours of sleep. The home show was tomorrow, and though Nicole said she had everything under control, Kayla wasn't so sure. It was a big event, the most important promotional gig of her career. Nicole had to be nervous. Kayla wanted to help her. She felt a strong pull to book a return flight immediately, but she felt an equally strong pull to stay in Sage Creek. Timber and Sophia needed her here.

She refused to be yet one more adult in their lives who walked out on them when things became inconvenient or hard.

With a huff, she got up and grabbed her computer from the dresser. She tried logging on. Nope. The hotel manager really needed to adjust their free Wi-Fi sign. Nonexistent internet was more like it.

Finally the connection went through and her emails popped onto the screen. Brenda had sent her a message. She clicked on it. Faith Owens had created some promotional materials to send to the Seattle stores. Kayla downloaded three brochure variations and a document filled with typed copy.

They weren't bad, but they weren't up to the standards that Seattle businesses would need. She glanced at the time on her screen. She'd call Noah in a couple of hours, once he and his clan had a chance to wake up. But until then, she'd do some investigating on her own. First step, to learn all she could regarding Helping Hands—their vision statement, unique heartbeat and success stories.

She navigated to a series of video clips at the bottom of the website's About Us page. Relatively well-produced footage followed, but they'd be more effective if Noah and his team dived deeper. Show the need, the challenges they faced when initiating life change. And, most important, where those men the ministry had helped were now.

Best place to start—with Noah himself.

She entered his name, followed by "bull rider," into her search-engine browser and spent the next thirty minutes learning practically all there was to know about the cowboy. Well, at least, all that was on the internet, which was a lot. The man had clearly downplayed his rodeo successes. He'd ridden in nearly every state, as far as she could tell, and had even placed in the National Finals Rodeo.

He also hadn't been exaggerating regarding his injuries. She started to watch a video from one of his bull rides, flinched and quickly closed the window. She clicked on a televised interview instead and was instantly drawn to Noah's strong confidence and rugged good looks. He hadn't changed much since his rodeo days—at least, not in terms of appearance. But, thankfully, a humility she found quite appealing had tempered the cockiness she saw in his comments to the news reporter.

She assumed her interactions with him accurately portrayed his character. She wanted to think so, but had to consider he might be presenting a side of him he wanted her, and the children's social worker, to see.

Then again, he was a ministry leader. That counted for something, though it also counted against him, considering all it potentially exposed the children to.

And if they moved in with her? Could she manage single parenting? Get the kids to playdates and doctors' appointments, and whatever else came with raising little people? If she could only watch them three days a week now, what made her think she could possibly handle them full-time once back in Washington?

But she wouldn't be doing it alone. She might not have the depth of community support that Noah did, but she'd always have day care. She'd figure it all out, just like the million other single moms juggling their careers and motherhood.

That would break Noah's heart, for sure. Was she willing to do that?

If it was in Timber and Sophia's best interest, then yes. But now wasn't the time to worry about all that. Focusing back on Noah's furniture pitch, she spent the next hour jotting down notes, ideas and questions.

She glanced outside. The sun had finally peeked over the horizon. After enough coffee to, hopefully, counteract her loss of sleep, she showered, dressed, made some phone calls, then headed to what she frequently used as a remote office—the Literary Sweet Spot.

The familiar scents of coffee, chocolate and cinnamon welcomed her when she walked in to what was quickly becoming her favorite location in all of Sage Creek, if not the entire Texas Hill Country.

"There's my long-lost friend." Leslie, a girl she'd hardly known in high school but had begun to form a friendship with, waved from behind the counter. "I thought maybe you were taking the day off."

She laughed. "That'd be nice. But I've got numerous video conferences today, a materials list to approve and some project proposals to send out."

"Sure would love to see what you can do." Leslie restocked fresh brownies into the display counter. "Figure it's about time I gave this place a redo."

Her best friend from high school, a local hairdresser, had been saying the same thing about her salon. "I could lay out some design options for you. But, unfortunately, I won't be around long enough to oversee the project myself."

"Sure. You know what they say about beggars being choosers, right? What do you want? Triple shot, almond milk, caramel—two pumps, no whip?"

"Perfect." That was something she'd missed about Sage Creek: how everyone knew—and for the most part, generally cared about—one another. If only she could find such a tight-knit community in Bellingham. Then again, she hadn't really tried. She'd always been too busy chasing her dreams.

Kayla paid for her order, waved to some of the ladies from Trinity Faith's quilting club and chose an empty table near the window.

Her phone rang. She glanced at the screen and smiled as an image of Noah's boyish grin sprang to mind. That man was too handsome for her own good. She answered. "Noah, good morning."

"Hey, Twinkle Toes."

Her cheeks warmed at the memory of her hand in his, the other on his strong, steady shoulder. His presence—and voice—always managed to calm her. "Oh, seems to me maybe you should own that title. Noah Williams, the two-stepping king."

"Don't go broadcasting that, now. A man's got to maintain his cover."

"It'd conflict with your bad-boy image?"

He chuckled. "Something like that." She could hear the whir of a machine, now getting fainter, in the background. "You ever been to the Little Tykes Barefoot Blitz?"

"I haven't but it sounds adorable."

"Timber keeps things lively, that's for sure. So you want to join us? We're heading there tonight for their toddler-parent romp."

Yes! She took a deep breath to rein in her obviously overinflated enthusiasm. Apparently skimming through all of Noah's past bull-riding photos had not helped her keep her heart in check. "I, um… When?"

"Seven o'clock work?" He paused. "I figured you'd enjoy the time with the littles—I usually bring Sophia along. To bond, you know?"

Right. Because her nephew still acted like she was a big ol' scary stranger, hiding behind Noah's leg whenever she came around. Which was absolutely the cutest—uncle and toddler.

If the Sage Creek ladies thought Noah was attractive before, they should catch a glimpse of him with Timber.

Then again, they probably had. Matter of fact, he likely had a string of women clamoring for his attention.

Women who planned to stay in Sage Creek.

"Kayla?"

"Huh?"

"Tonight. Want to come?"

Based on how much the idea excited her, it was probably the last thing she should be doing. Except she did want to develop a relationship with her niece and nephew, not to mention gauge Noah's skills as fill-in father. "I'd love to."

"Great. I'll pick you up at your hotel at a quarter to."

"See you then."

Not that things could ever work between her and Noah, a fact she'd do well to remember. But her thoughts kept drifting to him, of her and him together, making it difficult to stay focused on her work. By the time she made it back to her hotel that evening, she'd envisioned at least half a dozen romantic scenarios—strolling hand in hand, sharing an ice-cream cone while sitting on a park bench, galloping on horses across his property as the sun dipped lower on the horizon.

Kayla Fisher, you're pathetic, you know that? She huffed and grabbed her brush from the dresser. Though a few spritzes of hair spray helped tame the effects of Texas's summer humidity, she was in desperate need of a cut. Maybe she could talk Trista into fitting her in.

She could hear the sound of an engine. Then a door banged shut and heavy boots clomped to the door. Her pulse accelerated as a familiar flutter swept through her midsection. Taking a deep breath, she opened her door to find Noah standing on the stoop dressed in his signature Stetson, a teal T-shirt that accentuated the blue flecks in his eyes and faded blue jeans.

"You look good." He blushed and shifted. "I mean, I like that color on you. It's very summery. Is that a word? What I'm trying to say is…" He released a breath. "You ready?"

He was adorable when flustered. She smiled, fighting an unexpected shyness herself. "I am."

"How was your day?" He held the door of his truck open for her, then offered a hand as she climbed in.

His skin felt rough and scratchy against hers. "Good. Busy and filled with plenty of coffee, just how I like it."

"My kind of lady." He laughed, closed her door, then rounded the truck and climbed in on the driver's side.

Behind her, Timber jabbered in a singsong voice while Sophia made raspberry noises. Kayla rotated to face them. "Hi, big guy." He scrunched his face into the far side of his car seat. She laughed and gave Sophia's leg a squeeze. "And hello to you, little one. You have a nice afternoon?"

She squealed and kicked her feet, making Kayla laugh.

"Full of naps and mashed potatoes, the both of them." Noah eased onto the gravel road. "Since then, Timber's been convinced he's a T. rex and Sophia's been engaged in a continual game of 'let's drop the Binky.'"

"Were you being a stinker with your grandparents?" Kayla grazed a hand over Sophia's silky soft hair.

"That's what I heard." Noah cast her a sideways glance. "What about you? You get a lot of work done today?"

"Some. I spent most of my time in video conferences, but I managed to tackle a few things in between." She tucked a lock of hair behind her ear. "I went over the content Brenda forwarded me, too."

"And?"

"It's a good start." She shared her thoughts and ideas. "Who made your promo video?"

"You don't like it?"

"I'm not saying that. But I do think…well, I think we could do better."

He rubbed the back of his neck. "We hired a fella from Austin. He cost a pretty penny. Not sure we have the funds to get him back out."

She nodded and scraped her teeth across her bottom lip. "What about Trinity Faith? Do they have a video camera we can borrow?"

"Maybe."

"I'd love to interview some of the men you serve. Especially your success stories. I think that'll really help drum up some interest, you know?"

"I'm not sure we have the time for that. I meet with our lawyer next week. I'll need to write a check for his retainer then."

"Okay. No problem. We'll go with print material for now. But I think we could still use a story to share—the more dramatic, the better."

He scratched his beard, then gave a quick nod. "I might just have the perfect one. I'll make some calls tomorrow. I'm pretty sure I can get Jed's wife to write something up. You remember Paige Cordell? Well, Paige Gilbertson now."

"Those two actually got married?"

He nodded.

"Wow. I mean, I always thought they would, but then, after they broke up and Paige moved away. To Chicago, right?"

"For a spell. Seemed small-town living tugged at her, though."

Kayla could understand that sentiment. Sage Creek had a way of doing that to a person, and if not for her design firm, maybe she'd move back, too.

She felt as if her heart was being pulled in three different directions—toward Noah, the kids and the career that was finally just beginning to take off.

Chapter Ten

When they reached Little Tykes, Noah beat Kayla to the entrance. He set Sophia's car seat on the sidewalk and held the door open, clutching a squirming Timber in his free arm. "Hold on, little guy. The play equipment isn't going anywhere."

Kayla laughed. "Looks like someone's excited to be here." She wasn't sure what melted her heart more—Noah's gentle strength or Timber's uncontainable enthusiasm. Combined, those two made it nearly impossible for her to keep her wits about her.

She stepped inside, and Noah's earthy, citrus cologne swept over her. Hands on her hips, she scanned the area. "What a cheerful environment they've got here."

Children's music—lyrics about a mother and baby frog sitting on a log—played from speakers positioned in ceiling corners.

He plucked off Timber's shoes and socks, then lowered him to the ground. Timber immediately toddled toward a green, barrel-shaped mat. "Julia Nieves owns the place. She opened it up about a year ago."

"I remember her. She was a year younger than me, right? Blond hair, the greenest eyes ever?"

"That'd be her." He unlatched Sophia from her carrier. "Want to hold her?"

"I'd love to."

He handed over the baby.

Sophia immediately began to fuss. "Oh!" Kayla stiffened. "I'm sorry. What'd I do?"

"Nothing. She's been a bit moody lately. Hold her facing out, like this." He helped reposition Sophia in Kayla's arms. "And bounce gently. Babies love movement."

Kayla complied, and Sophia quieted. "You seem to know a lot about infants."

"Just what my mom and the internet have taught me."

"I love that baby smell. And her hair is so soft." She eyed him. "Regarding the childcare arrangement. Still need me on Mondays, Tuesdays and Thursdays?"

"Does that work for you?"

"Yep." Should she tell him she'd been looking into permanent guardianship and, should it ever come to that, legal adoption? Was she being deceptive by keeping her inquiries to herself? Yet, with so many unknowns still ahead, her decisions included, it didn't seem wise to stir up unnecessary conflict, especially considering she and Noah needed to partner together in all this. "That'll give me easy access to you whenever we wanted to talk your promo stuff. Kills two birds with one stone."

Plus, it'd keep her in shouting distance from Brenda, should she ever need her help, which Kayla for sure would. Other than the couple of Sundays she'd served in the children's nursery, she hadn't cared for children since her babysitting days in high school. That had been exhausting.

She'd hated every low-paid moment and, after about ten temper tantrums and toddler meltdowns, she'd determined, by the age of sixteen, that she never wanted children. Though her estimation of the munchkins had improved considerably over the years, she wasn't certain her ability to manage them successfully had.

But she was only committing to three days a week. Surely she could handle that. If not, better to discover that now, before filing for guardianship.

Out a window, she watched a young mom crossing the parking lot carrying a wiggling, clearly distraught little boy who looked ready to flail out of his mother's arms at any moment. The exasperated look on the woman's face reminded Kayla of the many nights she'd tried to get crying kids into bed during her babysitting days.

What if she discovered she was completely inept at this parenting thing? Or that she wasn't able to manage her business while raising them?

"Kayla?"

She startled and turned toward Noah. "Huh?"

He gave her an amused yet kind look. "I'm grateful for all you're doing to help my ministry. And I plan to give you a cut."

"I wasn't expecting that." Nor could his nonprofit afford that. Besides, all their efforts could amount to nothing but wasted time for the both of them.

"I know, but it's only fair."

"I appreciate the sentiment."

"And I appreciate you." The admiration in his eyes only made her want to help him more.

Noah crossed to where Timber sat playing with colored balls stored in an inflatable pool. Timber plunged one hand in, then the other, then pulled them out and squealed. Pretty soon, he started smacking at the balls, sending them flying while Noah scrambled to put them back.

A yellow one landed at Kayla's feet. "Seems you're

fighting a losing battle, cowboy." Still holding Sophia, she lobbed it toward his head.

Grinning, he darted out of the way. "Hey, now. A mite aggressive, are we?"

The door behind them chimed as a handful of women entered, little ones in tow.

"Hello, hello, hello!" Julia swept in wearing a violet polo shirt with a bright yellow sun in the center. "Is everyone ready to blitz, bounce and bop?" She mock-danced, and a few of the moms and their toddlers joined her. "Gather round, y'all. Find your shape and call it out."

Kayla glanced around. Noah was the only adult male in the room, but if that made him uncomfortable, he didn't show it. She admired his quiet confidence. After the last guy she'd dated—a hotel manager with a constant need to prove his masculinity—she found Noah's strong yet gentle demeanor refreshing.

Why was he still single? Because of his ministry? His past?

Was he commitment-shy? If so, he showed no signs of that, as far as the children were involved.

Timber scurried to one of the large green squares on the floor and jumped on it with both feet. "Scawe!" His voice merged with all the other, high-pitched exclamations, only a few clear and understandable.

Noah and Kayla took the open spots on either side of him, and soon everyone had formed a circle with the teacher in the center.

"You ready to get your wiggles out?" Julia jiggled her arms and legs, and all the children did the same. A toddler with rosy cheeks and curly red hair fell on her backside, and a little black-haired boy scampered off toward a stack of foam blocks. Though his mom scooped him up and brought him back, his escape seemed to trigger an adventurous spirit in a few of the kids, and soon moms and tykes were darting every which way.

Noah and Timber, on the other hand, appeared deeply engaged in a game of copycat. Timber would do something, like kick out one foot, and Noah would do the same. He'd study Noah for a moment. Then he'd flap his arms. This went on for a little while until Noah caught Kayla watching him. Then he quickly straightened, and his movements stiffened slightly.

Next, Julia pulled out a giant, rainbow-patterned parachute, and Timber scrambled to grab a handle. Everyone else did, as well.

Noah took an open spot next to Kayla. "You want me to take Sophia?"

She held the child close and kissed her neck. "Uh-uh."

He laughed.

Julia directed everyone to sit and "make waves," as she called it. Timber landed on the ground with a plop, legs extended in front of him. He giggled, and, with Sophia cradled in her lap, Kayla wrapped an arm around Timber's torso and gave him a squeeze. When Timber smiled up at her with those big brown eyes of his, she thought her heart might melt.

They fit together, the four of them, almost like they were a family, though it wouldn't do her any good thinking that way.

After parachute time, Julia announced everyone's favorite activity, based on the squeals she initiated: free play. Within moments, kiddos toddled off in various directions, most of them heading toward the ball pit. Timber followed a set of twins to large, log-shaped mats, and Noah and Kayla followed Timber.

Two other ladies stood a few feet away, engaged in conversation, from the sounds of it, on the frustrations of sleep deprivation.

"I don't know what's gotten into her." The smaller of the two, a woman with long blond hair streaked with purple, sighed. "She had been sleeping through the night. But all of a sudden, it's like her internal clock started waking her up around two o'clock for a middle-of-the-night play session. By the time I get her—and myself!—back to sleep, it's often after three. Two hours later, the baby starts fussing, wanting to wake up."

"I hear you. I don't think I've managed a full night's sleep since my first grader was born. My husband helps cover night duty on occasion, but as he likes to remind me, he can't 'nap all day'—" she made air quotes "—like I can." She scoffed. "He keeps bugging me about finding a job, but with how much day care costs, I'm not sure it'd be worth it."

That was something else Kayla needed to check into. As a small-business owner living from project to project, day care could be a problem. If only she and Noah lived in the same area, then they could tag-team it more. She could watch the kids a few days a week while working from home, and then maybe he could do the same. And Brenda could fill in when either of them had a conflict or important meeting or something.

Kayla studied Noah, his tender eyes and gentle, almost shy, smile.

She'd grown much too fond of that man. She was probably just relying on him for comfort and support during a time when everything felt uncertain. But once she returned home, with or without the kids, Kayla would soon forget all about him.

Wouldn't she?

Except that he'd probably want to continue seeing them, as would his parents. That meant she'd be interacting with him for years to come. She wasn't sure how she felt about that.

Actually, she knew all too well how she felt, and that frightened her.

Her phone pinged. She glanced at the text, then at Noah. "That's my assistant. Can you excuse me?"

He nodded, then followed Timber to a foam pit filled with laughing toddlers.

Kayla stepped outside, then called Nicole. "Hey, how are you holding up?"

"Honest answer?"

Kayla held her breath.

"Fabulously." Nicole laughed. "Now that we've moved past that whole pink-wall mess."

"You handled that well." Nicole had had the wall repainted and a major discount issued by the day's end, with a promise for a free redesign. Mrs. Ansel and her leery husband had both been more than pleased. "The home show, too. How'd your television interview go?"

"Great!" Nicole went on to tell how nervous she'd been, trying on half a dozen outfits, along with how she'd practiced answering imaginary questions to her reflection in the mirror.

"I'm sure you did wonderfully."

"Well, you'll know soon enough. The program airs this weekend."

"Wow. Seriously?"

"Yep. Plus, I've got another interview lined up for later this month, this one with a Seattle station."

"What? How?"

"I contacted a friend who knows someone connected with the morning show and pitched a design segment geared to viewers, helping them mix and match colors and patterns. I titled it Going Chic without Going Broke."

"That's awesome." And it was, but still, it stung. It wasn't that Nicole didn't deserve the limelight, especially with how she'd stepped up since Kayla had left. But Kayla had been working long and hard to make a name for herself. Their firm wouldn't have even made it into the home show if not for her years of hard work and networking. And now, when everything was beginning to come together, she felt so removed from it all.

"Didn't I tell you if you hired me, you wouldn't regret it?" Nicole asked.

"One of the best decisions I've made. Almost makes me think you don't need me."

"It is nice to know you trust me."

"I do." Or at least, she was learning to. "So you're okay if I stay longer?" Unfortunately, she had zero idea just how long that'd be.

"For sure. Do what you need to do."

"Any chance you'd be up to meeting with some potential clients? I sent some proposals out this morning. I need to follow up with requests for a few face-to-faces. I know you said you didn't want to do any sales…"

"I'd love to. This is all stuff I need to learn, if I ever want to own my own firm someday."

Her gut pinched. "I didn't realize that was your goal." What if Nicole decided to branch out on her own and took a chunk of Kayla's clients with her?

She did her best to add cheer and confidence into her voice. "Thanks for stepping up. I really appreciate you."

"Absolutely! We're a team."

Hopefully Nicole would remember that after her televised interview and all the prestige it brought her. "Send me your availability, and I'll schedule some meetings. I'll call you later to coach you up." And potentially equip her to leave that much sooner.

Kayla would just have to make sure Nicole had every reason to stay.

Chapter Eleven

Noah stood in what felt like a cavernous lobby of one of those fancy, multifloor office buildings. The arched ceilings, made of etched glass, were at least three stories high, and, facing the parking lot, tinted windows stretched from floor to ceiling. Long, tiled hallways extended on either side of the elevators. The green Up arrow lit up, and a moment later two females dressed in crisp dress suits stepped out, engaged in conversation.

"Excuse me." He moved out of their way, feeling a bit out of place in his scuffed cowboy boots and faded blue jeans.

Manila file tucked under his arm, he checked the number in his email against the directory embedded into the wall, then rode the elevator to the second floor. The law firm was at the end of a long hall lined with more doors and windows. A burst of cool air carrying the faint scent of leather swept over him as he entered. Sleek black chairs were positioned around a glass coffee table, and modern paintings, like those you might see in big-city art museums, decorated the walls.

"Good morning." A woman with long black hair and red glasses offered him a formal smile. She sat behind a marble counter decorated on each end with fresh flowers.

He approached with a tip of his hat. "Good morning, ma'am. I have an appointment with Mr. Brymer."

"Your name?"

"Noah Williams."

She picked up her phone. "Mr. Williams is here to see you, sir." She'd barely hung up when a door to her left opened, revealing a short, heavyset man with round wire-rimmed glasses and wavy gray hair.

"Mr. Williams, come in." Mr. Brymer motioned toward his office behind him.

Obliging, Noah greeted the man with a firm handshake. "Morning, sir."

The man crossed the room and sat behind a large mahogany desk, signaling for Noah to take an overstuffed leather chair in front of him. "How was your drive into the city?"

"Not bad." But knowing this fella was likely charging by the minute, he couldn't afford chitchat. "I brought a check for the retainer." He handed it over along with the agreement letter he'd printed out and signed. "Thanks for taking our case."

Mr. Brymer nodded. "You brought the information I requested?"

"I did." He set down his manila file, filled with all of Ralph's work history. "Fortunately, we documented most everything, including our one-on-ones and his performance-improvement plan. We tried to work with him and gave him every chance to get himself together."

"Tell me about your history. When did you hire him on?"

Noah rubbed at his thumb knuckle. Elliot had warned him not to hire him, said the guy was too unpredictable, too entitled and ungrateful. Said he hadn't shown clear signs of rehabilitation. Noah had disagreed, certain the man just needed someone to believe in him and give him a second chance. "Less than a month after he finished the program. Ralph was in dire straits financially, and I let my compassion override my good sense. Looking back, I made way too many allowances for his behavior."

"Where did he work prior to Helping Hands?"

"He'd been in our program." He explained his ministry's rehabilitation strategy. "For a while, he was doing real good. Oh, he had his hiccups, for sure, but he made significant progress, enough that I felt he was ready for steady employment. I guess I wanted to give him a shot. It can be hard for these guys to get a job, especially if they've got a rap sheet." Which Ralph did.

"You offered a position to a high-risk employee."

Noah nodded.

"That could help us. Makes you more sympathetic, for sure. Then again, it could hurt us, too." He jotted notes on a legal pad. "You indicated he originally appeared to be working out?"

"For the most part. But then maybe three months in, he began to change. Started coming in late, getting defensive over every little thing. Losing his temper. I'm pretty sure he started using again."

"Did you confront him regarding his behavior and your suspicions?"

"Yeah. I was planning to have him drug-tested, but before I could, he lost it while working with one of our band saws. He cursed, called my right-hand man names I'd rather not repeat here, threw the wood he'd been cutting and stormed off. Next day, when he showed up, I handed him his final paycheck and asked him to leave. Told him not to come back unless he wanted to get cleaned up and work the program again."

"I take it he wasn't interested."

Noah scoffed. "Hardly. The dude was a hothead who had no intention of following rules or procedure. We can't have that. We let our staff know, before we hire them on, that they're to set an example in everything they do. Honestly, I don't see how the guy has a case."

Mr. Brymer nodded and, after giving Ralph's files a once-over, rubbed the back of his hand under his chin. "You're right—he doesn't have much legal ground to stand on. But that doesn't mean he won't try to drag this thing out, force you to settle."

Noah released a heavy breath. "Either that or go under."

"You think he has a personal vendetta."

"I know he does."

Mr. Brymer set down the folder. "You've got two options. Settle now for as low as you can, which honestly might save you money in the long run, even if you end up winning. Or fight this."

Helping Hands didn't have the money for either. "Mind if I pray on it some?"

"Not at all. In the meantime, I'll contact Ralph's lawyer to let him know to send all correspondence to me. That alone might scare the guy into backing down."

"I hope so." He sat taller. "You need anything else from me?"

"Not at this time. I'll review these documents and will be in touch."

At two hundred dollars an hour. But what choice did they have?

Lord, we're looking to You here. You started this ministry. I have to believe You'll keep it afloat.

* * *

That afternoon, Timber seemed to have an extra dose of energy and greatly decreased patience, so Kayla decided to take the kids to the playground. Located a few blocks from downtown Sage Creek, it boasted a tunnel slide, teeter-totter, merry-go-round and geometric jungle gym.

The air felt hot and sticky and in need of a good rain. Kayla searched for shade. Not finding any, she released Timber's hand and placed Sophia's baby carrier on the ground. "You want to build a sandcastle?" She pulled some plastic cups and spoons, which would serve as shovels, from her diaper bag and held them out.

Timber just looked at them, then shifted to watch two older children scamper up a rock wall leading to monkey bars.

Kayla tugged out a sheet from under all the other gear she'd brought, a massive amount of snacks included, and spread it on the ground. "Come on, little princess." She unfastened Sophia from her carrier, laid her on the sheet and positioned a few of her toys around her.

Her phone chimed a text, and warmth spread through her as her thoughts shifted to Noah. Apparently his meeting was done.

She started to reply then called him instead. "Hey. How'd it go?"

"Expensive and guaranteed to become even more so the longer this deal drags out."

"What are you going to do?"

"Pray."

Poor Noah. Caring for his orphaned niece and nephew, managing a ministry that, as far as she could tell, had been struggling, and now facing a costly lawsuit. He had to be feeling the pressure.

"I gotta tell you, this really stinks," he said. "I invested in that guy. Stuck my neck out, convinced everyone else, despite their better judgment, to take him on. It almost feels like I'm fighting for my brother all over again."

"Think that's why you did it? Hired Ralph, I mean?"

"Could be." He scoffed. "With all my talk against becoming an enabler, here I am, paying the consequences for doing the very thing I teach others not to do."

"You didn't know how everything would turn out."

"I guess. Listen, I've got to let you go. See you tonight?"

Funny how much she liked the sound of that. "We'll be there. And come hungry, because I've got pot roast simmering in the Crock-Pot."

Silence followed. Did he find that odd? Think she was trying too hard? That she was maybe pushing for something beyond this whole childcare-sharing arrangement? She probably shouldn't have said anything, and certainly shouldn't have spent all morning preparing dinner.

"That sounds amazing," he said. "Because I'm starved."

After she hung up, she replayed their conversation in her mind, especially his delayed response and how it'd made her feel. She was getting too attached to him, precisely what she'd determined not to do. *Kayla, keep your distance, girl.* She couldn't let her heart become entangled in something that could never be.

Considering the amount of time they'd been spending together, that wasn't going to be easy.

A car door behind her banged shut. She turned to see Trista stumbling toward her in a cute purple sundress and strappy sandals that, clearly, made it difficult to navigate the uneven grass. Halfway to Kayla, she nearly tripped and spilled the blended coffee she was carrying.

"Hey there." She gave Kayla a side hug then handed

her a drink. "Sorry I'm late. One of my clients suddenly decided she wanted highlights and lowlights."

"But you come bearing treats, so all is good." She took a sip of her drink, the cool liquid sending a delicious shiver through her.

"I talked to Leslie."

"And?"

"She's pretty set on having you decorate that place of hers. She's convinced it'll help business, make the Sweet Spot more of a hangout than it already is."

"She told me. She wants to draw in the younger crowd."

"Yep."

Kayla sat on the bench and watched Timber jump on and off the bottom step of the playground.

Trista sat beside her. "I told her I'd talk you into helping out your old friend, so long as you agreed to redesign my salon first."

"You know I probably won't be here long."

"Keep telling yourself that, love." Trista gave her a knowing smile.

"What are you saying?"

"Oh, nothing." She tugged her straw up and down then took a drink. "But I will have a spare room in a week or so."

"You're finally kicking your roommate out?"

"Oh, I was about to, but she beat me to it. Said she got a job in Ohio. Which means…" She angled her head. "Sure beats staying in a hotel. Matter of fact, maybe we could work out some kind of a deal. I give you free room and board, and in exchange, you give me a whole new salon."

Kayla crossed her arms. "Why do I feel like you're getting the better part of the bargain here?"

"How you figure?"

"You get a free remodel, and in exchange, I have to put up with you."

Laughing, she gave Kayla a gentle shove. "Just think about it. Because you and I both know you'll be in Sage Creek for a while."

It was looking that way. And if not for her business, she might even consider staying long-term. Making a life for herself here, with the kids.

And Noah?

Chapter Twelve

Kayla checked her reflection in the rearview mirror, fluffed her humidity-limp hair and added a dab of gloss to her lips. Then chastised herself for going through the extra effort. Though she tried to deceive herself into believing she was simply trying to appear professional for a meeting, her jittery stomach indicated otherwise.

When had it become so important what Noah thought of her? She hadn't been this distracted by a man in some time, and that only seemed to be increasing the more time she and Noah spent together. Common sense told her to take a step back, to add some distance between the two of them, but obviously, she couldn't do that. Not if she wanted to stay involved in Sophia's and Timber's lives.

And helping him with his ministry's financial struggles? That was simply the right thing to do.

With a deep breath, she stepped out, locked her car and strolled, shoulders back, toward the bookstore. The bell above the door chimed as she entered, and the enticing scents of yeasty cinnamon and coffee swept over her.

"Hey there." Leslie, who stood wiping a table, grinned at Kayla. "I'll be with you in a minute."

Kayla nodded and scanned the dining area for Noah.

He sat across from a petite brunette with olive-toned skin. That must be Faith Owens, she thought. She had her laptop opened and angled so they both could see the screen.

Kayla checked the time on her phone and, assured she still had a few moments before their meeting, ambled to the café counter.

Leslie met her at the register. "Triple shot, almond milk, caramel—two pumps, no whip."

Kayla smiled. "You remembered." Evidence of how often she made this place her office.

"Of course." She rung Kayla up, took her credit card, then handed it back with her receipt. "I'll bring it out to you, along with a slice of apple-cinnamon streusel bread. Frequent-customer perks—you get to try out my culinary inventions before I unleash them on the public."

"That sounds lovely, thank you." It warmed her heart how quickly and easily everyone had welcomed her back and made her feel as if Sage Creek was home.

Draping her purse over her shoulder, she approached Noah's table. Faith saw her first and stood to greet her. "You must be Kayla, the brilliant interior designer and businesswoman Noah's told me so much about."

Kayla's gaze sprang to Noah, and the admiring look in his eyes brought a surge of heat to her face. She cleared her throat and shook Faith's hand, then Noah's. "He exaggerates, I'm sure."

"Oh, I don't know about that." Faith tucked her hair behind her ears and sat back down. "Your sales-expansion ideas just might be the thing to save Noah's ministry."

She fought a frown at the reminder of all that was at stake. Somehow those stakes felt higher having Noah involved than they would've had he been any other client. Because of the kids? In part, for sure, and she refused to analyze her emotions further.

"Have a seat." Noah pulled her chair out then returned to his. "We were just brainstorming life-change stories."

"Great!" Kayla grabbed a notepad from her bag. "Would you mind if I helped with the selection?" She didn't have a marketing degree, but she'd taught herself a lot about generating media attention, a social-media buzz and creating client buy-in. "But first, can you tell me more about the ministry?"

"What would you like to know?" he asked.

"Why'd you start it?"

"From gratitude more than anything else. I told you some of my story the other day."

She nodded.

"I wasn't too keen on moving back in with my mom, and I wasn't sure what I thought of her married to another man. I expected him to be like my birth dad. I figured out pretty quick he wasn't the wife-beating kind, but I still didn't trust him. Kept trying to figure out what he was after."

"I can understand why."

"He proved to me some folk are just good men, simple as that. And he's one of them. Kind and gentle, but firm and stubborn as a thirty-year-old mule when he needs to be. Like when I thought I could return to my bar-hopping ways."

"He wasn't a fan, huh?"

Noah released a gust of air. "That's one way of putting it. First time I came home drunk, he met me at the door. Told me he loved my mama something fierce. Said if I wanted to throw my life away, that was my choice, but he was tired of seeing my mama all torn up. Wanted to know, then and there, if I really loved her. I told him I did, and he said he didn't believe me. Said no one could love their mama and treat her how I was."

He shook his head. "I didn't know how to respond to that. So I just sat quiet for a bit, thinking on what he'd said. I knew in my heart he was right. The next morning, he woke me up at six o'clock, like I was some punk kid in high school, which was exactly how I was acting. Told me if I was going to stay in his house, I'd need to earn my keep. Took me to his shop that very day and showed me how to be a real man—one who knows how to work hard and take responsibility for his actions."

"And the rest is history."

"Something like that. Though the journey's been challenging, we've seen a lot of guys completely turn their lives around. Now to figure out a way to get to them *before* they hit rock bottom and hurt their loved ones in the process."

She flipped to a clean sheet in her notepad. "All right. You said you were working through success stories?"

Noah nodded. "I spoke with Paige, the writer married to one of my buddies, earlier this morning. We narrowed our options to three, maybe four, testimonies." He handed Kayla a sheet of paper with the name *Darrel Simms* typed on the top and underlined. "His parole officer sent him to us, and let me tell you, he wasn't happy about it. He thought he could just come in, do his time, toss out a few snarky comments and be done with it all. But we make our guys sign a life progress plan agreement, or LPPA."

Kayla read the bulleted notes. The man had been a lifelong drinker who began experimenting with drugs in middle school. By eighteen, he'd become hooked on crystal meth. Kayla shook her head. "Seems like he developed quite a rap sheet. Stealing from his family, his friends, his boss, his employment."

"Yeah." Noah took a sip of his drink. "That's not uncommon. A lot of these folks, they're spending one hundred, two hundred dollars on their habit. Some of them can manage that for a while, but then they lose their job, get arrested—or both—and their income stream stops. So they turn to stealing or selling or a bunch of other things."

Kayla's eyes pricked as she thought about her sister, where she might be and what her addiction might've driven her to. *Lord, help her. Please. Whatever it takes. Bring her to her knees so that she'll find You.*

"So what made him turn around?" Faith asked.

Noah shrugged. "I guess just working the program. When men come into our system, they agree to certain things—attend group therapy, practice good self-care, work in the shop making something useful and participate in weekly Bible studies." He smiled. "Pretty sure God used that last piece to grab hold of Darrel's heart."

Kayla raised her eyebrows. "He agreed to all that?"

"Didn't have much choice," Noah said. "It was that or break his parole. Course, we have a lot of former inmates come for similar reasons who never change. They do what they've got to do, provide the right, rehearsed answers to all the right questions, then leave and go back to their self-destructing lifestyle."

Faith frowned. "That's so sad. How many end up staying clean and sober?"

"Statistically speaking?" Noah rubbed the back of his neck and gazed across the room as if mentally calculating. "I'd say maybe thirty percent."

Kayla's heart sank as she once again thought of her sister. "That's not a very hope-filled number."

Noah's eyes softened, and for a moment, he held her gaze.

"Sad statistics, for sure." Faith shifted. "But we're here to talk about Helping Hands' wins." She shuffled through her papers. "I think Cameron West's story will have more impact. It's amazing he's not dead."

Kayla shifted through her sheets until she found the name. She scanned the page while Noah read off the main points. "The guy who stole from his supplier? Seriously?"

Noah scoffed. "Yeah. Real smart, huh? He figured they wouldn't call the cops on him, which was true. But apparently he forgot who he was dealing with. I mean, all addicts put their families in danger, the minute they start using. But Cameron brought family endangerment to a whole new level."

"How'd he break free from them?" Kayla asked.

"The man he'd angered ended up going to jail. But by then, Cameron's life had spiraled into the gutter. His wife got pretty freaked out, told him that with everything he was bringing into their lives, the people that kept coming around and whatnot, that it wasn't safe for the kids. She up and left, and took their children with her. He lost his family, his job and, shortly after, his home."

Noah continued sharing Cameron's story, but Kayla's mind was stuck on the part about the drug dealers. Helping Hands dealt with some really rough men—men who, potentially, had angered a lot of people.

With Timber and Sophia living one hundred or so yards away.

But what was the alternative? Noah's mom couldn't take them, not full-time, not while caring for her husband. And Kayla's grandparents were getting too old. They might have enough energy now to keep up with a toddler, and that was a big maybe. What about when Timber and Sophia hit their teenage years?

Kayla was the only reasonable alternative.

She needed to figure out what it would take to gain legal custody of those children. Just in case, though the probability of her becoming a single parent was seeming more likely by the day.

By the time Noah arrived back at Helping Hands, most of the men from his afternoon discipleship group had beat him there. He smiled. That was good. It showed their progress. Initially, everyone had arrived late, some considerably so. He'd spent a good deal of time coaching them on character, and honoring one another's time had been a huge part of that.

"Good to see you all." He deposited his papers from his marketing meeting on Brenda's desk and inhaled the scent of fresh-brewed coffee. "Whoever made the coffee, my sleep-deprived brain cells thank you." He headed toward the kitchen, pausing to give a few fist bumps and man hugs along the way.

Jason McClellan, the oldest in the program, followed Noah. "Did you get my message about Hugh?" The sides of his mustache extended past his mouth and his silver goatee covered most of his chin.

Noah pulled a mug from the cupboard. "I did. I listened real quick while heading into a meeting but haven't had a chance to do more than that."

"I worry he's in a real bad place."

He nodded and poured steaming coffee into his mug. "He still seeing his assigned mentor?" Noah, with the help of Pastor Roger from Trinity Faith, paired each of his guys with a mature Christian.

Jason shrugged and pulled a soda from the fridge. "He missed a few. He told me he had conflicting appointments or some such thing, but I'm not sure how legit his excuses are."

"I'll talk to him." If Hugh chose not to follow the program, Noah would have to cut him loose. That was one of the hardest parts of his job, but like his dad used to say, can't help a man who won't help himself.

"Appreciate it."

Noah clamped a hand on Jason's shoulder. "And I appreciate you. You've come a long way, my friend." Used to be, Jason didn't care about anyone but himself. He was always on the defensive, thinking others were out to get him or slight him. Now he was not only driven by empathy for his brothers, but he was also showing signs of leadership. Noah'd be wise to find ways to nurture that gift.

But, of course, he needed to act with caution. The ministry certainly didn't need another Ralph on their hands.

The men ambled back into the living room. Brenda had arranged folding chairs throughout the room, interspersed between the couch and armchairs.

Noah sat with his back to the window. "All right, y'all. Tell me your wins for last week." He glanced from face to face. "You want to start us off?" He nudged the guy to his right, a bony thirtysomething-year-old with deep-set eyes and large ears that poked out from beneath his ball cap.

"Sure." The guy leaned back and crossed his arms. "Let's see. I had to deal with my ex last week. That woman has a mouth on her that could blister a sailor's ears." He whistled, and the other men laughed. "But I remained cool as a tomato slice fresh from the icebox. Just looked her in the eye, let her rant—"

"Make a fool of herself is more like it," Jason said.

"For sure." The guy chuckled. "But not me. Matter of fact, I think I shocked her some, I stayed so calm."

Noah grinned. "That's awesome, Tim. What do you attribute that to?"

He shrugged. "Guess all your talk about stepping into

manhood and trusting God to have my back is finally sinking in."

"Good to hear it." Noah gave him a fist bump. "So to break that down for the other fellas, you realized God would fight your battles—"

"And do a much better job of it than I ever could—without the mess I always cause when I let my temper get the best of me."

"What about after?" Noah asked. "Were you tempted to drink?" One of the hardest challenges these men faced during recovery was learning to feel. Some of them had spent years, decades even, numbing their emotions with drugs and alcohol. Once they cleaned up, a lot of them didn't know how to deal with all the inner turmoil, be it daily frustration or pain from past trauma.

Tim rubbed the outside of his hand. "Sure, it crossed my mind. Mainly 'cause that was my MO for so long, and like you're always telling us, old habits can be hard to break."

"But you didn't," Noah said.

Tim grinned. "No, sir. Not one drop. Though I did take my frustrations out hacking up some logs on my property."

"Good." Noah smiled. "That's a healthy way to deal with emotions." He made a visual sweep of the other men. "Who else is ready to share?"

For the next ten minutes, as he guided the others into sharing their celebrations, he reminded the guys of how far they'd come and verbally reinforced each of their self-care steps. He'd learned a long time ago the power of calling out other people's strengths. Not only did that bolster a man, but it also acted like an object lesson for everyone listening.

When they'd finished, he grabbed their work order

notebook from the shelf and explained their needs. "We don't know if these stores will take our merchandise, but we need to be prepared for if they do. And maybe a few of you who've been with us for a while can help train our newbies."

"We got this." Jason made a fist pump.

Noah laughed. "I believe you do." But he'd still need to find more man hours. Even if all his guys were all in and made zero mistakes, they still wouldn't be able to produce the inventory they needed.

Noah needed to call Drake and see if they couldn't wrangle up their old buddies to help.

Chapter Thirteen

By midmorning, Timber had turned fussy and feisty, almost as if he was intentionally trying to frustrate Kayla. She took a photo of him with her phone—him on his tiptoes, straining for the remote she'd placed on the table—and sent it to Noah, with the text Someone is going stir-crazy!

Thankfully, Sophia seemed content sitting and cooing in her bouncy seat. Now if only Kayla could find something to keep her brother equally happy, before he broke out into a tantrum. What did all the other moms in Sage Creek do during the week? She ambled into the kitchen to make a fresh pot of coffee, then searched for indoor children's activities while she waited for it to brew.

A site titled "Help for the Frazzled Mom" captured her attention and led her to numerous articles, one in particular that seemed promising.

Her phone chimed a text. It was from Noah. Take him outside and have him run?

She replied: I think I've got a better idea. Do you have any extra sheets?

If he found her question strange, he never indicated, but neither did he have any spare bedding.

Kayla texted back: No problem. I've got an idea. She dropped her phone on the counter and headed to the bathroom, running a hand over Timber's soft head as she passed. "Hold on, little man." A few moments later, she'd covered a large section of floor with towels laid edge-to-edge and placed a glass baking dish half-filled with rice in the center. "You want to come play?" After motioning over Timber, she added utensils, a cup and bowl, some penne noodles and a few toy trucks to her makeshift sensory area. Then she took another picture and sent it to Noah.

He replied with a laughing-face emoji and the text So you're trying to force me to vacuum, I see.

Their banter, and knowing they were working together, felt good. It'd gotten to the point where they were communicating multiple times a day, like how a husband and wife might. Not that Kayla was looking for that type of relationship.

Besides, Noah might not stay so cordial, should he learn she was strongly considering filing for custody. Though she hated to think her actions might harm their relationship, she had to do what she felt was right. She at least needed to investigate the matter and determine her next steps.

While both children spent the next thirty or so minutes happily entertaining themselves, Kayla researched all the legalities related to kinship adoption. After she'd accumulated three pages' worth of notes, she set them aside to quickly skim her email inbox. Most were from work, some were spam and one was a playdate invite Lucy had forwarded.

She clicked on it, glanced at the time and smiled. "Perfect." Sage Creek moms were meeting at the local park in just over an hour, which gave Kayla just enough time to sift through the half a dozen invoices and estimates Nicole had cc'd her on.

The number in the third proposal, which had been sent to lawyer John Kollings, didn't seem right. She scrolled back, read through all the line items and tapped on her phone's calculator app. A sinking feeling hit her gut. Swallowing, she added the numbers again, then a third time.

She called Nicole.

Her assistant answered. "Good morning. I thought we shifted our phone meeting to tomorrow."

"We did, but…" She took a deep breath and released it slowly, willing her tone to remain calm and friendly. "In Mr. Kollings's estimate, you transposed two numbers."

"What? Are you sure?" Nicole paused, and the sound of typing followed. "I'm so sorry. Oh, Kayla, I can't believe I did that. I was in a hurry, heading out to meet one of our clients, and thought I could knock some to-dos off my list first. I totally should've slowed down to double-check my calculations. I'll send him an email to explain."

That was a huge error. A fifteen-thousand-dollar error. "If we lose this client, it could cost us more—not just in his business, but in our reputation, as well."

"What do you want me to do?"

"I'll take care of this. But you can pray that he shows us grace and doesn't think we're unprofessional." Though she always strove to honor her word, people made mistakes, and this was an honest one. Surely he'd understand.

Kayla shouldn't have allowed Nicole to handle this case. She'd given her too much to manage in too short of a time frame. "Anything else?"

"Other than my massive blunder?" She gave a sheepish laugh. "Nope."

"All right. I'll call you tomorrow."

She ended the call and set her phone on the table.

She needed to get back home soon, before her business fell apart.

And bring the kids with her?

"All right, you little rascals." She closed her computer. "How about we hit the park?" She needed some fresh air and sunshine to give her brain time to catch up and formulate a plan.

"Pawk?" Timber sprang to his feet. "Me go!" He toddled to her, arms in front of him. "Me go, too, pwease."

She smiled, scooped him up and held him close. "Do you have any idea how much joy you bring me?"

She arrived at the playground to find about a dozen moms gathered in groups of three and four. Some sat on the bench, others on blankets spread over the grass and still others circled the equipment as their kiddos climbed up the stairs, then went down the slide.

"Hi." Kayla tucked her fingers in her pocket and looked around. Two toddlers, likely near Timber's age, sat, foot-to-foot, in the sandbox. One of them, a curly-haired little girl, scooped sand with a shovel then dumped it. Her friend watched, then mimicked her.

"Aren't they adorable?"

Kayla turned to see Sammie, a girl with whom she'd gone to school but never interacted with much, standing beside her holding a baby.

Kayla, holding Sophia, smiled. "They are."

"Us moms have been meeting for going on five years now. It's been really fun to see all the relationships our kids have developed. Sort of like a big extended family."

Kayla kissed the back of Sophia's head, her gaze shifting to Timber. She remembered what it was like, growing up in a small town, knowing when you went to the park or the candy store, you'd likely meet a friend. Or, at least, someone would be by pretty quickly. She remembered Sunday-evening prayer service, how bored she used to get, and how Doris Harper used to always slip her pieces of bubble gum.

Her grandma had always said Sage Creek was a great place to raise a family. Kayla agreed, but it wasn't the only place. Bellingham had churches and moms groups and playgrounds. Kayla would just have to make a point to get connected.

If she received custody.

Once again, she thought of the pain doing so would cause Noah, and her heart pinched.

If only there was some way he'd move or they could somehow split the kids' time between them, like if she took them during the school year and they spent their summers in Sage Creek.

Only that wouldn't save the issues related to his ministry.

It felt as if she'd landed in an impossible situation, one where someone was bound to get hurt.

With his midmorning meeting canceled, Noah used his unexpected free time to run a few errands. He stopped at the bank to transfer funds from his savings to cover a check. They needed to start selling furniture soon. He made a mental note to follow up with Kayla regarding their pitches to Seattle businesses, then climbed back into his truck and headed toward the office-supply store.

As he passed the park, he caught a glimpse of a brunette sitting on a bench holding a baby. Was that...? He took a closer look, then scanned the playground for Timber. He saw his little buddy bouncing on a metal-spring turtle.

Noah smiled as an idea emerged. Ten minutes later,

he returned with a flavored latte for Kayla, black coffee for himself and pastries for the both of them and Timber. She must've seen him approach, because she turned to face him. Initially, her eyes widened, but then she gave him that smile he'd grown to love.

"What are you doing here?" Her gaze dropped to the drink tray and the bag he carried, then back to his face.

"Was out and saw you and the wee ones milling about." He handed over her drink. "Triple shot, almond milk, caramel—two pumps, no whip."

Her eyebrows shot up. "How'd you…?"

"Leslie told me."

She laughed, and the most adorable pink spread through her cheeks. "Thank you." She took a sip, then cast him a sideways glance, as if trying to figure him out.

Truth be told, he was doing the same—trying to figure out how this sweet woman had captured his attention so. Had him running across town to buy her favorite drink and, once he saw her, like he had today, rearranging his schedule just so he could spend more time with her.

When he had clearly spent too much time with her already.

Not to mention he was more than a little out of place, at the moment, as the sole man crashing a mother-child play-date. Though he'd considered coming on more than one occasion, if only to get Timber out and around other kids.

If Kayla stayed, if they raised the children together, she could do that.

Like she was doing today.

He lingered for a bit, attempting to join in on the conversations going on around him, though most centered on difficult in-law relationships and dealing with unsolicited parenting advice. He was about to excuse himself when the other ladies started collecting their munchkins to leave.

"You up for a walk?" He motioned toward the walking-path/bike-trail that extended from the edge of the playground and wove through the residential area behind. "I've got Timber and Sophia's stroller in the back of my truck."

"You come prepared," Kayla said.

"I try."

"Though it's getting close to Timber's nap."

"They can both sleep while we walk."

She nodded, and the two of them gathered the children's things. "So how did your phone meeting with the lawyer go?" She loaded Sophia into the stroller, and Noah hooked in a groggy-eyed Timber beside her.

He frowned. "Seems to me everything's just dragging along about as slow as they can go. Nothing's changed. The guy still doesn't have a case—at least, that's what my lawyer keeps telling me. But that might not matter. I might spend all our money before we even get to court."

"I'm sorry."

"It is what it is."

"I'll contact a few more Seattle boutique owners this afternoon."

"Appreciate it."

They walked in silence for a moment, him pushing the stroller while she strode beside him. He could sense, by her slow step and the way she stared at the ground in front of her, that something was wrong. "Hey." He cast her a sideways glance, tempted to grab her hand. "You okay?"

She released a soft sigh. "Yeah. I just… My assistant made an expensive blunder, and this after a series of other issues. First, a paint that was supposed to be a blush dried cotton-candy pink and we had to pay our crew to repaint. Then we had a client go ballistic once the tile layers started laying her flooring. And now… Financially, I feel squeezed, and I haven't figured out how to fix it."

"Probably doesn't help, trying to manage everything from some five states away."

"Right." She plucked a leaf off a nearby bush. "We're quite the pair, huh?"

He gave a weak laugh. "Guess so." He glanced down at Timber and Sophia. Both had fallen asleep. "Want to sit?" He motioned to a shaded area beneath a mature oak.

"Okay."

A butterfly flitted in front of them before landing on a nearby flower. "What're you doing tonight?"

"Besides spinning myself into an anxious mess?"

He laughed. "Yeah, besides that."

"Nothing. Why? Do you want me to watch the kids?"

And there was his out. He could change his mind, keep his mouth shut, and she'd never be the wiser. Except he'd never been a coward, not even around a confident, beautiful woman. "Actually, I was thinking of asking my mom if they could spend the evening with her."

"Oh?"

He swallowed, his throat suddenly scratchy. "One of my buddies and his grandmother own our local dinner theater, and he asked if I'd come check out his new show. I guess he switched things up a bit. Not sure I really want to go alone. Plus, he could probably use a woman's opinion, anyway." Though that was all true, it wasn't his motivation for asking her.

He held his breath, trying to read her expression. Would she think his invitation had crossed a line?

"Um, sure." She smiled. "That sounds fun."

The air swooshed from his lungs. "Great." He fought the grin threatening to take over his face. "I'll pick you up at six."

Chapter Fourteen

Kayla stared at her meager selection of clothing, spread across her bed. If only she'd done laundry last night, like she'd planned.

She glanced toward the hallway, half tempted to do a load of wash right now, but there wasn't time.

With Noah Williams. Her stomach dipped. She could hardly believe she was going out with Noah Williams, perhaps the best-looking cowboy in all of Texas.

She could hardly believe he'd asked her. Did that mean he found her attractive?

No. His reasons had been purely logical.

Still, she should've declined his invitation, based on the way her pulse spiked the moment he asked her. Not to mention her goals as far as the children were concerned. Getting more entangled with the man clearly determined to raise them would only muddle her thoughts, and thus her decisions, further.

With a huff, she plucked her least wrinkled outfit off the bed and put it on. Then, dressed in a rainbow-striped romper that hit just above her knees, she grabbed her brush and faced the mirror.

She was badly in need of a cut and color.

As if on cue, her phone chimed. Trista had forwarded a silly video, asking her to coffee.

Kayla mouthed a thank-you to the ceiling and shot off a response. How about I bring coffee to you, in exchange for a cut and color, with highlights?

Trista texted back: Ha! That must be some coffee! Add in a salon makeover, and you've got yourself free hair appointments for a year.

That would be quite a deal, if Kayla were planning to stay that long. Regardless, considering how great a friend Trista was, Kayla agreed. Let me know your next opening, and I'll be there. She doubted Noah would mind accommodating whatever date Trista suggested. Worst-case scenario, she'd ask one of the ladies from Trinity Faith Church to watch the kids.

Of course, this arrangement did little to help her limp locks today. With a sigh, she grabbed her hair spray, hung her head upside down and spritzed. She stood up straight again and scrutinized her reflection, satisfied with the increased volume. After freshening up her makeup, she still had fifteen or so minutes to spare, so she sat on the edge of her mattress and opened her laptop.

No surprise, the Wi-Fi proved too weak and intermittent for her to log in to her email, so she spent the rest of her time brainstorming solutions to their current design challenges. They had three home redesigns lined up within the next month, two that involved structural changes. One of their clients wanted stained cement in their basement, and another was hoping to add a minibar and theater alcove.

A knock sounded on her door, making her jump.

Noah. A jolt shot through her. Taking in a slow breath to calm her ricocheting emotions, she closed her computer and stood. She took one last glance in the mirror, gave her hair one more fluff, grabbed her purse and answered.

"Hey." Noah grinned and tipped his hat to her. "You look…" His Adam's apple dipped. "Nice." He wore his signature faded blue jeans, gray boots and a teal T-shirt that brought out the blue flecks in his gray eyes.

"So do you." That statement couldn't have been truer, though entertaining such thoughts wouldn't help her any.

He moved aside and motioned toward his truck behind him. "After you."

"Thank you." She stepped into the humid evening air, catching a heart-skipping whiff of his citrus cologne. "Where's this dinner theater at?"

"About ten minutes from here, in an old strip mall." He opened the truck door for her. "Hope you're hungry, because they're serving pitchfork rib eye—apparently a signature dish—and smoky mac 'n' cheese."

She raised an eyebrow. "Pitchfork rib eye?"

He shrugged. "Probably a regular cut with some special seasoning his grandma thought up. She's always inventing new recipes and has the talent to actually pull it off." He grinned, closed her door, rounded the truck with a slap to the engine, then climbed in. As usual, the radio was playing, but he turned it down. "You get any work done this afternoon, after I took the kids?"

"Not really." Between the law-firm remodel and this date—which wasn't a date—she'd struggled to focus. "But I did send out some more emails pitching your furniture."

"Oh?" He turned onto the two-lane highway heading toward town.

"I figured might as well put the time waiting to hear back from the others to good use." Unfortunately, two store owners had already declined, almost immediately.

"Any idea as to when we should expect responses from the others?"

She shook her head. She didn't have the heart to tell him that they might not ever, that no reply was often an answer in itself. "I'll send follow-ups out in a few days or so."

He nodded, lines etched into his forehead.

Poor guy. His stress level—with the lawsuit, raising the kids, trying to keep the ministry afloat—had to be wearing on him. Unfortunately, she understood precisely how he must feel. Only she was carrying the added guilt of knowing, depending on how things went with her guardianship inquiries, that she was about to break his heart.

Matter of fact, she almost felt deceptive, going on this dinner date—which was positively not a date!—with him tonight. Maybe if she reminded herself of that, her insides wouldn't turn so jiggly whenever his gray-blue eyes latched on to hers.

"How long did Timber end up sleeping this afternoon?" Kayla asked. Noah had decided to take them to his parents' house after their park date, since he wanted to ask his mom to watch them for the night anyway.

"He woke the minute I transferred him to the truck and was a bear the rest of the day."

"I'm sorry."

"It was hilarious, actually. I swung through the store to grab snacks and whatnot for them to eat at my mom's. I let him push one of those kiddie carts—that normally keeps him occupied for at least two grocery aisles. But then he started throwing random stuff into his cart."

"Junk food?"

"You'd think, but nope. Strange stuff, like canned beans, noodles, a big ol' bag of dried lentils. I told him to stop and that we needed to put it all back. Probably should've just let him keep going and dealt with unloading it all later."

"I take it he wasn't pleased with your suggestion."

"Ha. Hardly. He plunked down on his rear, right there in the middle of the aisle, crossed his arms, scrunched up his face in the most ridiculous scowl I've seen and refused to budge. I figured, no biggie, I'd just pick him up, throw him over my shoulder and finish shopping. That triggered the loudest temper tantrum I've seen, one that got his sister wailing soon enough. The way he started flailing all about, and with me still trying to push his sister in my cart, I thought for sure I'd drop him."

"What'd you do?"

"Made a fool of myself, that's what." He chuckled. "I started acting like a horse, galloping up and down, him on my shoulder, while trying to steer the cart straight without plowing into any of the gawkers. And let me tell you, there were more than a few of those."

"And Timber's cart full of the food you didn't want?"

"Left it right there, like I maybe should've done the first time."

She laughed. "What you're telling me is, the next time I need to go shopping, find a babysitter first."

"That about sums it up, yep." He turned into the parking lot for a gray, partially vacant strip mall. The dinner theater, which had a Wild West exterior with its name burned into a sign of rough-hewn wood, stood sandwiched between an office-supply store and a craft-and-fabric shop.

"This is it."

She glanced around at the handful of cars in the nearby stalls. "Is this a private showing?" She wasn't sure how she'd feel about that, if it was. The idea felt much more intimate than she'd been anticipating.

"Nah. We're early. So my buddy and his wife can give us the lowdown before everyone shows up."

She nodded and stepped out, a brisk wind stirring her fluffed and sprayed hair. So much for all her primping and prepping.

"I hope you enjoy the show." He reached the door in two long strides and held it open for her. "It's supposed to be funny. And romantic."

She thought she saw red inch up his neck, but then he cleared his throat and hurried inside.

Was he attracted to her?

"Oh, my goodness!" Though her wavy red hair had lightened some, and she wore it longer than she had in high school, Kayla recognized Paige immediately. The woman swept her into a strong hug. "Kayla Fisher! I haven't seen you in ages. How've you been?"

They chatted briefly. Paige wanted to know all about her life on the West Coast in home design, and Kayla asked her questions regarding her writing career.

"I thought you were working in Chicago or something." Kayla surveyed the lobby, feeling as if she'd stepped back in time. She saw Noah's design touches in nearly everything, from the counter, made from a thick slab of wood, to the rough wood paneling.

"I was." Paige led the way into a dining area filled with tables and chairs, each set slightly different, but all similar to the ones she'd seen in Noah's workshop. The guy was crazy talented. She'd known that before, but seeing his work here, all together and in a room designed to match...

She caught his eye. "This is impressive."

Blotches of red climbed his neck once again, and he averted his gaze. "It was all my buddy's idea."

His shy, almost boyish side was absolutely adorable.
Too adorable.

"Where's Jed?" He looked around. "Back in the
kitchen sampling all the food?"

Paige laughed. "You know him all too well." She
pulled two sheets of paper from a clipboard on a nearby
table and pencils from her back pocket, then handed one
of each to Kayla and Noah. "Again, thank you both so
much for coming. We crave feedback! As you can see,
we've listed a bunch of questions, but we've also left
space for general comments or suggestions. And please
be honest. We can't get better otherwise."

She smiled then glanced at a clock on the far wall.
"Now, if you'll excuse me, I need to check on the cast real
quick to make sure they understand their lines."

"Happy to oblige, aren't we, Kayla?"

Right. He'd invited her to help his friends, not to tug
on her heart.

Maybe focusing on the survey in front of her would
help her remember that—distract her from the tall, handsome cowboy standing dangerously close to her.

Noah was captivated by Kayla's response to the play—
the way her face lit up when she laughed, and her head
tilted, with tiny lines etched above her brows, whenever
something triggered her curiosity. And the way she took
notes throughout, not just for Paige and Jed's feedback
survey, but to actually solve the mystery, reminded him
of the studious girl he'd encountered back in high school.

He'd always felt an attraction to her but figured she
was way out of his league, because back then she had
been. While he'd been barely passing, she'd made the
honor roll. Most likely, on all the nights he went searching for a party, she stayed home studying. And while

he'd dated—if you could call it that—practically every cheerleader in the county, he couldn't remember her having a single boyfriend.

Oh, wait. She'd spent time with that quiet kid in biology. What was his name?

She looked over, catching him watching her. "Is everything all right?" She set down her pencil.

He quickly covered with what he hoped she read as a jokester smile. "Absolutely. Just…you know…" He leaned over her paper in an exaggerated way. "Just eyeing your sleuthmanship."

"You're wrong!" A cast member's voice jolted his attention back to the play. "You're all wrong!" The woman, wearing a puffy red gown with black lace, thrust her fisted hands down at her sides. "I'm innocent, I tell you! I'm innocent." She ran off the stage crying.

Jed walked onto the stage dressed in a period costume. "Do you believe her or do the clues point to someone else? In a moment, we're going to serve dessert. While we do, work together at your tables to determine who did it and why."

Chatter filled the room as guests shimmied closer, leaning over their notes, and talked out clues and theories.

"What do you think?" Kayla's eyes danced with a childlike pleasure that made him want to pull her close.

With a mental shake, he cleared his throat and straightened. "That Albert dude seemed pretty shady, and he had plenty reason to kill that guy. He blamed him for his failed ranch, thought he'd been swindled, and that James practically had the sheriff in his pocket."

"Meaning he may have felt as if he didn't have much choice." She tapped the end of her pencil against her chin. "But with how Alice was acting, sneaking around, always popping up at weird—"

Loud clanging sounded in the kitchen, and talking stopped as everyone turned toward the noise. They soon resumed their sleuthing, Kayla included. Though Noah offered occasional suggestions, his focus remained on the beautiful woman sitting beside him.

He startled at a hand on his shoulder and looked up to see Jed standing above him with a worried expression.

"Hey," Noah said. "What's up?"

Jed squatted between him and Kayla. "I'm probably a jerk for saying this, especially considering the only reason you two came was to help Paige and I out." He spoke in a low voice. "But we just dropped a tray full of desserts on the floor. We've got enough leftovers from last night and the night before to feed most everyone, and we'll do a pretty fruit plate for those who are gluten- or dairy-free. I realize that doesn't apply to either of you..."

"I can't speak for Kayla, but for myself, I say, bring on the melons." Noah grinned, hoping his enthused voice would allay Jed's concern.

Kayla nodded. "I'm fine with that. I can go without, too. Whatever you need."

Jed released a breath, his worry lines smoothing into a smile. "Thanks, you two. You're the best." He stood and darted back into the kitchen.

Twenty minutes later, everyone had been served, the killer had been unveiled and almost all the guests had filtered out. The few that remained were perusing various trinkets displayed in the gift store.

"Thanks so much for coming." Jed shook Noah's hand then Kayla's, and his wife gave them both a hug.

"I hope our feedback helps," Noah said.

Paige glanced at the pages they'd given her. "Oh, I'm sure they will, and if there's ever a way we can return the favor…" She shifted to Kayla. "If you need me to write advertising copy for you or anything, just let me know."

Kayla smiled. "I will, thanks."

Noah gave his friend a final tip of his hat then rested his hand on the small of Kayla's back. "Shall we?"

She nodded and let him guide her out into the inky night. Stars glimmered against an indigo sky and a half-moon peeked through wispy clouds. The air held a slight chill, as if rain hovered on the horizon.

Reaching the truck, he opened the passenger-side door for her. "You know, we never did get our dessert."

"But they served us fruit."

"Like I said, we never did get our dessert."

She laughed and settled into her seat.

"I say we need to rectify that." He closed her door before she could respond, then added, once he'd slid into the truck, "You up for some ice cream?"

"Always. But I doubt Simple Sundaes is still open." She glanced at the time on her phone. "Don't they close at ten?"

He frowned, cranked the engine and stared straight ahead, one hand on the wheel. Then he grinned. "Probably so, but the grocery store doesn't." He backed out, turned his truck around and headed toward Main Street. Less than ten minutes later, he parked in the Piggly Wiggly lot, flashed her a boyish grin and hurried inside.

Kayla was left sitting in Noah's truck, feeling like a schoolgirl on her first date, because this date-that-clearly-wasn't-a-date was beginning to feel very much like one. Worse, she welcomed the idea.

Kayla Fisher, what are you doing?

Noah pulled into the hotel parking lot, lit by a single dust-dulled streetlight and a faint glow radiating from the lobby.

"Um… What're we doing here?" Kayla sat stiffly, her features tight.

"Having us some dessert." Why did she seem so nervous all of a sudden?

"I'm not comfortable inviting you into my room."

"What?" He half laughed, half exhaled. "Of course not. Thought we could sit under the stars a bit." He motioned toward a set of chairs outside that were positioned on either side of the front doors.

She studied him with a furrowed brow, as if not understanding.

"Come on." He opened his door, grabbed the grocery bag and got out. "You'll see." Gravel crunched beneath his boots and he heard her door thud closed.

She met him near the chairs and waited, hands clasped in front of her, while he rearranged them so that they were closer together.

"You're not cold, are you?"

She shook her head and brushed windblown hair from her face.

"Have a seat." He motioned toward one of the chairs then sat beside her. He pulled a small box of plastic spoons from his bag, then a pint of ice cream. "Rocky Road, right?"

"How'd you know?"

If he told her, would she think he was a creeper? "I saw something you posted on Facebook."

"I don't remember posting anything about ice cream."

He scratched the back of his neck and shifted in his chair. "It was a couple weeks ago. I sort of stalked your profile a bit." Initially, curiosity drove him, but it hadn't taken long for her sweet smile and laughing eyes to pull him in.

"That's okay. I stalked you, too."

"Oh?" He raised an eyebrow.

"I needed to see what kind of environment Timber and Sophia were living in."

"Oh." In other words, her interest didn't go beyond that, beyond them. If only he could say the same, then maybe his heart wouldn't be dipping and leaping with every conversation shift.

He pulled off the lid of the ice cream and handed her a spoon. "Mind if we share?" He probably should've bought bowls, but he'd had this whole image in his mind. Thought maybe this would be romantic, when he had no business thinking that way in the first place.

"I don't mind at all." She ate a spoonful, then leaned back and stared up at the night sky. "It's so quiet, so peaceful. Not that Bellingham's all that busy or loud, really, but… It's so beautiful out here. Without all the city lights drowning out the stars."

It was beautiful, and so was she, on the inside even more than the outside. She was smart, talented, great with the kids.

Why couldn't he meet a woman like her in Sage Creek? Someone who would love those kids as if they were her own? Someone he could form a family with?

He rested an ankle on his knee. "You miss it?"

"Texas?"

He nodded.

"Sometimes. The people, mainly. Being able to walk into the coffee shop, or Wilma's, or even the grocery store, and run into someone you know. Maybe even someone who helped raise you, at least on Sunday mornings and evenings."

"Feels good, knowing Timber and Sophia will have that. Knowing when they're in the nursery, they're being held by the same ladies that held me when I was their age. Or when it's time for them to go to Sunday school, that they'll get to be loved on by Lucy and her crew, and, God willing, if she's still around, Ms. Doris included."

"I get it, believe me, I do. But one thing to think about… What will it be like for them to live in the same town with their drug-addicted mother? Wanting to be with her but knowing they can't? I mean, don't get me wrong. I hope and pray my sister will get better, but you know the statistics."

He did, and he'd seen many a family destroyed by drugs. "What are you saying?"

"Have you ever considered moving? Giving them a fresh start?"

"Like where?"

She shrugged and offered a slight smile. "Washington State's always an option."

His heart stuttered. He couldn't lose Timber and Sophia. "If you're thinking those kids might be better off somewhere else, you're wrong. I know seeing their mama around town might hurt, but losing a whole community that loves them would hurt them a lot worse. You've got to know that."

Chapter Fifteen

The next morning, Kayla arrived at Noah's place at five minutes before nine.

He answered the door before she had a chance to knock. "Morning." He moved aside and motioned her in. "Can I grab you a cup of coffee?"

Timber poked his head around Noah's legs. She smiled and waved at him. Then he made a vrooming noise and darted off.

She stepped inside. "That sounds lovely, thank you."

With a nod, he rounded the Formica breakfast bar separating the tiny kitchen from the living area and pulled a mug from the cupboard. "Milk and sugar?"

It touched her that he always seemed to remember so many details about her—like her favorite type of ice cream and how she took her coffee. "Heavy on both, thank you." She crossed to where a cooing Sophia was lying on a blanket on the floor. "Morning, princess. You ready to spend the day with Aunt Kayla?" She gave Sophia's pudgy big toe a gentle tug.

Toy cars were littered across the rustic-looking coffee table, an array of children's clothes covered the floral couch and Timber's favorite blanket was draped over the vintage rocker.

Noah sidled up beside her and handed over a steaming cup.

She took a sip of coffee and closed her eyes. "Mmm. Perfect." She paused. "I really appreciate you letting me be part of the children's lives like this."

"Always. So long as you don't go sneaking off with the kiddos." His eyes searched hers.

Almost as if he knew she was leaning toward guardianship more each day. Most likely, he'd been analyzing their conversation from the night before, maybe even had come to share her logic.

He stepped closer and lifted her chin so that her eyes met his. "Stay here, in Sage Creek. We can raise them together. This is working out, right?"

Her heart squeezed. How she wanted to say yes. "If only it were that easy."

"It can be."

Tears stung her eyes, and she turned to face the window.

His footsteps retreated, paused, then shuffled into the kitchen. She turned back to watch him, wishing for something to say. He fiddled around, tidying up what didn't really need tidying, packed a travel lunch bag. "Timber might pester you about seeing the horses. He's already asked me half a dozen times to go see them."

He turned to Timber, who'd migrated into the room pulling a wooden train set by a string. Noah dropped to one knee and enveloped the tyke in a hug. "You be good, you hear? And come see your uncle for lunch." His gaze met Kayla's.

She nodded.

Noah stood, crossed to Sophia's blanket and lowered to kiss her forehead. "That goes for you, as well, little missy. No spitting up on your aunt's pretty blouse." He paused, angled his head. "What? You can't help that? A likely excuse."

He tickled her under her chin, then grabbed his lunch and ambled to the door.

Kayla followed, and he held her gaze with an almost pleading look, as if he wanted her to stay, and not just to help with the children. But his emotions were probably just jumbled, with everything that was going on with the kids and all. That was probably where both of their feelings came from. They were drawn to a common cause and felt a connection because of that. But that didn't mean they could make it as a couple.

They were nothing more than two friends linking arms during a difficult and confusing time.

Friends. The word stung. Her heart wanted more. She hadn't realized just how much until now.

After he left, their conversation replayed through her mind again and again. She got so lost in her thoughts she poured Timber's juice all over the counter instead of into the cup. While she was less than amused at having to mop up a sticky puddle of grape juice, which was likely to stain, Timber thought the situation hilarious.

His laughter triggered hers, which only made him giggle all the harder. He started hopping around the room.

"You're a bundle of energy this morning, aren't you?" She poked him in the ribs as he jumped past. "What do you say we blow this Popsicle…er, juice stand? Trade it for horses?"

Timber squealed and stomped his feet. "Hossie! Hossie!" He dashed to the door, plopped on his backside and attempted to shove his tiny feet into his still-tied shoes.

"All righty, then." Kayla ruffled Timber's hair then

dropped to her knees in front of him to help him out. "Kinda goes easier when you match the right shoe to the right foot."

Five minutes later, she had Sophia tucked securely in the baby backpack she'd found and they were traipsing down a dirt path toward a barnlike structure she assumed housed the horses. To the left, horses grazed in a large, fenced-in pasture area. To the right stood Noah's ministry, his workshop about five hundred yards south of that.

When they neared the pasture, Timber bolted ahead. "Wait." Kayla hurried after him, Sophia bouncing in her backpack, and grabbed his wrist moments before he reached the fence. She'd forgotten how fast little legs could go.

Unexpected movement in her peripheral vision startled her. She spun to see a large, heavily tattooed man walking along the expanse of grass between the stalls and Noah's workshop. He wore a black T-shirt, dark jeans and combat boots. Though the sun behind him shadowed much of his face, his body language suggested he was angry. Tense.

He stopped when he saw her, and she held her breath, suddenly feeling vulnerable with Noah and his staff and who knew who else inside a closed barn with loud machinery. She knew the type of men Noah's ministry served, how many of them were ex-cons and addicts, of which this man quite likely was. Why was he out here, roaming around?

"Dude."

She jumped at the sound of another man's voice, coming from her right. She turned to see a tall, muscular guy in jeans and a red workman's apron tied around the waist approach.

Upon seeing Kayla, he nodded, then pivoted back to the angry guy. "You have a chance to chill out?"

Pulling Timber to her, she faced the pasture, pretending not to pay attention to the conversation behind her while her ears remained pricked.

The bigger man sighed loudly. "Done told you I don't got time for some snotty-nosed mouth-off."

"Yeah, well, part of working the program means learning to get along with others."

"The punk should be glad I didn't knock that smirk right off his face. Leave him crawling around in the sawdust, looking for his busted-out teeth."

She flinched and nudged Timber. "Let's go, bud." She spoke quietly. "We'll come back later." When Noah was around.

Timber grunted a cry and shook his head. "Hossie! Hossie!" He reached toward the pasture, opening and closing his hand.

"I know, bud. I wish we could. We'll come back."

This wasn't the best environment for the kids. Or for her, for that matter.

Noah leaned back in his desk chair and folded his hands on his stomach. "You think we need to cut him loose?"

Elliot popped his knuckles one at a time. "Not sure. He's wound pretty tight."

"A lot of guys are when they first start coming. They haven't learned how to handle their emotions in a healthy way."

"Yeah, but they usually listen when we try to coach them."

"Not at first." Noah knew what Elliot was implying, and he might be right. Maybe the man was unreachable, but they had to give him a chance. "Not always."

"What if he and Caleb had come to blows?"

He tugged on his trimmed beard. This was always the hardest part of rehabilitation ministry—knowing when to give grace and what for, and when to draw hard lines. "You talked to him? Explained the rules and behavior expectations?"

Elliot nodded. "Not sure he listened, though." He paused. "Kayla and the kids were out, hanging around the horses. She seemed pretty spooked. Think she had reason to be?"

Noah released a breath and scrubbed a hand over his face. "I'll talk to him."

Elliot stood. "Good enough."

At lunchtime, Noah popped home to see Kayla and the kids. The scents of fried chicken and fresh-baked biscuits greeted him as he walked in. Along with Sophia's steady wailing. Kayla was rocking her while Timber played with his plastic dinosaurs, apparently unperturbed.

Kayla, on the other hand, looked frazzled. "Yay. You get to see what an amazing nanny I am." Her laugh sounded forced.

"She gets like this sometimes. How long's she been crying?"

"I'm not sure. Fifteen minutes?"

"She was fussy off and on last night." He touched the back of his hand to her forehead. "She might be coming down with something."

"Should you call her doctor?"

He frowned. Should he? Truth be told, he'd never dealt with a sick infant before. "I don't want to jump at every cold. But I don't want to ignore something that's potentially serious, either."

"How do we know which is which?"

"We ask my mom." He pulled his phone from his back pocket, and within minutes, she'd given him a list of things to watch for and ways to quiet her down. "She told me to call back in half an hour if she's still upset."

"Wow. That feels like a crazy long time."

"Think some fresh air might help?"

"Maybe."

He turned to Timber. "Come on, little man. Let's slip on your shoes."

Timber scrambled to his feet. "Hossies?"

He winced, remembering what Elliot had told him about his interaction with Parker. "Sure, bud. We can swing by the stable for a minute."

He wrestled Timber's sandals on, then held the door open for him and Kayla. He followed them out and fell into step beside her while Timber toddled on ahead.

A breeze swept over them, and Sophia's cries settled into a slow whimper, then a sniffle.

He grinned. "Well, I'll be. Guess the girl didn't want any fried chicken, huh?"

Kayla laughed. "Ouch. Are you making a statement regarding my cooking, Noah Williams?"

"Course not. Haven't tried it yet." He smiled, enjoying their playful banter.

"Hey." She elbowed him in the side. "You better be careful if you want any leftovers for dinner."

"Now, there's a threat able to silence a man."

They paused as Timber got sidetracked jumping back and forth across a dried-up mud puddle. Then Kayla took in a deep breath and told him what he already knew—she'd had a not-so-pleasant encounter with Helping Hands' newest member. Though Noah couldn't even call the man that, as he was still in the probationary, prove-you're-serious-about-life-change phase.

"I heard," Noah said. "I plan to call him in for a one-on-one first thing tomorrow."

"These men you counsel—they've got a rough past, and most of them don't want to be here. Right?"

"Some. Some come voluntarily, directed to us by their pastors or counselors or whatnot. Others not so willingly as a term of their probation."

"What did he do?"

"To get arrested, you mean?"

She nodded.

"Check forgery, stolen credit cards, stuff like that."

"Better than what I was afraid of, but still."

"*Still* what?"

"I don't like it. Guys like that hanging around."

"I'd never put you or the kids in danger."

"Not intentionally, but I doubt you know your clients well. What if they have a violent streak, or maybe decided to rob your house someday and—"

He laughed. "You have seen it, right? The elegant exterior and fancy furniture?"

"I'm just saying."

He placed an arm around her waist and gave a gentle squeeze. "You and the kids are fine. Will be fine. I'd never let anyone hurt you." He turned her toward him, his gaze locked on hers, and took her hands in his. Man, was she beautiful. "Never."

In fact, he'd do everything in his power to bring her nothing but joy.

If she'd let him.

Chapter Sixteen

Standing in the center of his workshop, the scent of cedar wafting from the floor, Noah shoved a hand in his pocket and faced his buddies. The five of them, three former football teammates and two friends from church, formed a horseshoe in front of him. "I really appreciate you all giving up your Saturday to help me out."

"Got to take care of our own, isn't that right, Big D?" Jed, his friend who co-owned the dinner theater, smacked Drake Owens on the arm.

Drake adjusted his hat. "So long as Ms. Brenda's treating us to some of her famous fudge brownies, I've got all day. And next Saturday, and the Saturday after that." He glanced toward the supplies Noah had stacked along the wall. "How many tables and chairs you want us to make, anyway?"

"As many as we can with what we got." They couldn't afford to keep much of a surplus of material. Up until now, they'd always replenished what they used, as the money came in. But they needed to build up their inventory, in case one of Kayla's contacts came through. And if not…? They'd be out a whole lot more than rent money.

"You want us to form something like an assembly

line?" Drake approached the pile of logs, half of which were already debarked. "One of us can knock out a bunch of mortise joints. Jed here can make the tenons. You thinking an inch and a half for both?"

Noah nodded. "I'm good with however you fellas want to handle this."

"You know…" Jed rubbed the back of his neck. "I'm pretty sure Mrs. Watson's got a bunch of wood we could use out at her place. I heard she's looking for someone to help trim back her trees."

"Yeah, but are they any good?" Drake grabbed a debarked branch that was six inches in diameter. "Word has it she's got a bad case of oak wilt infecting her property."

"No reason we still couldn't use it," Jed said. "The fungus only grows on live trees, and whatever damage it caused would only make the wood look more rustic."

"Regardless, I'm not sure we have time." At least, Noah hoped they didn't, because if they did, that also meant Helping Hands wouldn't be getting any sales coming in. "Right now, I'd like to focus on making what we can with what we've got. After that, we can talk about approaching Mrs. Watson."

It'd be awesome if Kayla's idea took off as a long-term thing and the ministry started supplying stores throughout the country. The Bible said God turned bad things to good, and Noah was trusting Him to do the same with this lawsuit.

After divvying up roles, the men got to work, and by that afternoon, they'd completed two full table-and-chairs sets.

Jed stepped back, hand resting on his shiny belt buckle. "Not too shabby, if I do say so myself."

"It's a start." Noah calculated, roughly, how many more pieces they'd be able to make and about how long it'd take them. Hopefully they'd move faster as they went along.

Soft footsteps sounded behind him, and he turned to see Kayla standing a few feet away. Her worried expression concerned him.

"Fellas." He excused himself and crossed to where she stood. "Hey. Everything all right?" The kids were with his mom, so it couldn't be anything to do with them.

"Yeah. I…" She took a deep breath and released it slowly. "I heard back from our last contact. They sent me an email."

His stomach soured, but he fought to keep his expression blank.

"I'm sorry."

He scrubbed a hand over his face. Now what? He and his board had tried everything else they could think of to bring in funding. He could apply for a bank loan, but the best that could do was buy him time. If they lost this case, or even if it dragged on, like their lawyer suggested it would, they'd go under.

Maybe they should settle, except that would still wipe them clean. Matter of fact, they'd probably have to liquidate some of their equipment.

That was probably what Ralph wanted—to see this place fail. And for what? Because Noah had given him a second chance, fought to hire him on, tried to help him?

He released a heavy sigh. "Give me a minute."

She nodded, and he returned to thank his friends. He relayed what Kayla had told him and what it meant.

"Dude, that stinks," Drake said. "You want us to finish up here, just in case?"

"I don't want to waste your time."

"No waste." Jed grabbed a self-feeding drill bit. "God will find a use for these when He's good and ready."

The question was, would that be before or after Helping Hands tanked?

"Can you all give me a minute?" He needed a moment to think. To pray. He started to walk out, but Kayla hurried after him and fell into step beside him.

They walked in silence, gravel crunching beneath them, then soft earth as they continued past the stable and onto one of the trails his horses had long since forged across his property.

When they reached the fence line, he leaned against the corner pole and released a breath. "You ever feel like everything's coming against you all at once?"

"Sometimes." Her voice was soft, as were her eyes.

"I never thought I'd say this, but I might lose my ministry."

"Maybe that's for the best."

His jaw clenched. "What do you mean?"

"I'm not trying to be insensitive. It's just…well, things have changed. For the both of us. And sometimes when new things come, God rearranges us. He closes old doors so we can walk through the ones He's opened."

"Timber and Sophia?"

She nodded.

Of course, she would think closing Helping Hands was for the best. He knew how she felt about the place. But without it, what would he do? He still had to support himself, and if he was going to spend his time earning a paycheck, for sure he wanted to do something he loved.

There wasn't much he loved more than being a part of life change.

"I'm sorry." She placed a hand on his arm. "I know this hurts."

"It is what it is."

"Can we pray?"

He gave a half nod and bowed his head.

"Lord, I know You have a plan for all this—for Noah and how You want to use him, for the kids, for me." Her voice cracked. "What may feel like helpless or dark situations are merely opportunities for You to shine. Show us Your heart, and help us to trust in You. With all of this and whatever lies ahead."

"Amen." His tone turned husky, and he cleared his throat.

He stood there, watching the tall grass wave in the breeze and the trees beyond sway ever so gently. She stepped closer and leaned her head against his shoulder, and he opened an arm to let her in.

She fit snugly in his arms, her head tucked beneath his chin, her cheek against his chest and her hand, as light as a windblown leaf, on his arm. He'd stay like this forever, holding her close, if he could.

His phone rang, and he wrestled it out of his pocket. He didn't recognize the number. "Hello?"

"Hi. Is this Noah Williams?"

"Speaking."

"This is Amanda Southerland. I tend bar down at the Brew Hub."

"Okay?" Why would she be calling? He hadn't been to that place since his rodeo-chasing days.

"This probably sounds strange, but can we meet for coffee? To talk about your lawsuit. I've got some information I think might be important."

His stomach tightened. How did she know about it? What kind of garbage was Ralph spewing now, and if not him, one of his low-life friends? Noah wouldn't put it past the guy to gather up some witnesses in his favor, promising a cut if they testified on his behalf, or threatened to.

Wouldn't that just be the perfect ending to a disappointing day? "When?"

"You free now?"

He pulled the phone away from his ear to check the time. His mom had been minding the little ones all day. Though she'd insisted on watching them, she was likely ready for a break. He held the phone against his thigh and met Kayla's inquisitive gaze. "Think you can watch the kids for a spell?"

"Of course."

"Thanks." He was half tempted to send this gal directly to his lawyer, especially considering, for all he knew, she could be trying to swindle him. But his curiosity got the best of him. He returned the phone to his ear. "Sure. I can be at Wilma's in about fifteen."

He hung up.

"You need to go?" Kayla asked.

He nodded, and as they walked back, he relayed his conversation.

The wind stirred Kayla's hair in her face, and a few strands got stuck in her eyelashes. She smoothed them away. "It could be good news," she said.

"A man can hope."

Kayla slowed her rocking and glanced down at Timber. After nearly an hour of throwing a fit, the tyke had finally fallen asleep. He was turned toward Kayla with his pink mouth slightly parted and his chubby little hand resting on her collarbone.

This child stirred everything maternal within her—a longing for family she hadn't realized she'd had. "I don't think I can leave you, kiddo."

An image of Noah, leaning back against the fence-line post, staring straight ahead, came to mind, making her heart squeeze.

If only he'd move to Washington. What if God was setting him up for that? She hated to see him lose his ministry, knew how much it meant to him, but surely the kids meant more.

And her? What did she mean to him? Would he move for her? Surely he could find work in Bellingham, maybe even start a new ministry.

She glanced at the time on the DVR. There was no telling when Noah might be back, but with both kids asleep, she at least had a few minutes to work on guardianship stuff. She'd called a few day cares. Their fees had about squeezed the air from her. How did people afford it? She still had two more numbers to call, and though they weren't as close to her firm, they seemed pleasant enough. If the pictures on their website were any indication.

Carrying Timber, she tiptoed down the hall and into the nursery. Sophia was lying on her side, sucking her thumb, one hand tucked under her cheek. Her tiny torso rose and fell with every breath. Kayla watched for a moment, then crossed to Timber's bed, laid him down and tucked the blanket up under his chin.

Then she returned to the living room and positioned her opened laptop on the coffee table. She pulled out her sheets of notes. In order to gain legal guardianship, she needed to show the children had an attachment to her. She could do that, although they were closer to Noah. But not hugely, right? It wasn't like they'd been staying with him that long. Kayla had flown to Texas as soon as she'd heard about her sister's disappearance.

Still, they were currently living with Noah Williams. Did that mean, if she filed, the court would automatically rule in his favor? What if the state decided not to conduct a home study at all? What if they felt the children were better off with Noah?

All she could do was move forward, let the courts decide and trust God to work everything out as He saw best.

The first step was to document her concerns, including the men coming and going at Helping Hands, most of whom had a record. Writing it all down, she couldn't help but feel as if she was betraying Noah. But she feared she'd be betraying the children if she didn't, and they needed to be her main priority.

She had to be honest. Completely open. How else could the court make an informed decision?

Chapter Seventeen

Noah held the door open for an older couple as they exited Wilma's, then stepped inside and breathed in the scents of fried chicken and strawberry-rhubarb pie. He made a quick visual sweep for Amanda but didn't see her.

Lucy and some of her bridge-club friends sat at a table midway along the far wall. A couple of ranchers occupied two other tables, and a pair of high-school girls sipped milkshakes near the window.

"Hey there." Sally Jo, the owner's daughter, flashed him a smile. "Should I bring you a Coke, light on the ice?"

He smiled. "Thanks." He sat in the center of the dining area, facing the door. Seemed odd Amanda hadn't beaten him here, considering he'd driven in from the far edge of town. Had she changed her mind?

He was just about ready to leave when she pulled up in a gray two-door, then parked along the curb and hurried inside. Dressed in flannel shorts and a baggy T-shirt, with her long hair pulled up in a messy bun, she looked like she'd just rolled out of bed. Then again, she'd likely worked late the night before.

She glanced around, made eye contact, then strode

toward him. "Hi." The chair legs screeched against the linoleum flooring as she plopped down across from him. "You eating?"

"Hadn't planned on it." He wasn't sure he could stomach much of anything right now, after the way his day had been going and, based on this little meeting, could continue.

"Mind if I do? I'm starved."

"Go ahead." He resisted the urge to fidget or drum his fingers on the table while she scoured the menu. Either she was stalling or she was one of the few Sage Creek residents who didn't know everything Wilma's offered by memory. As soon as Sally Jo had taken her order, he crossed his arms and said, "So what's this about?"

Her face lightened a shade, and she took in a visible breath. "Like I told you when I called, I tend bar at the Brew Hub. Been there for going on two years now. I work most every Friday and Saturday night, and I've heard a lot of stories. I guess once people get to drinking, they forget I'm there, or maybe they don't care I'm listening."

"Okay." Where was this headed?

"Last night, Ralph came in, probably around seven or eight. I'm not sure, because we were pretty busy, and I was the only one there, you know? At first, he kept to himself, but then, after ten or so beers— Look, I know I should've cut him off."

He encouraged her to continue with a wave of his hand.

"Anyway, he got sloshed and started chumming it up with this other guy, a dude I hadn't seen around much before. The two of them got into some sort of rap-sheet competition, trying to prove who was tougher, I suppose. They started talking about all the bad things they'd done, how many people they'd riled up, what they'd been arrested for."

This conversation wasn't heading in the direction he'd thought it would. Though leery to hope for anything positive at this point, his gut no longer felt so tight. Still, so far, she hadn't told him anything he didn't already know. The fact that Ralph had a record would weaken his credibility, for sure. But not enough to get him to back off the lawsuit.

She glanced around, then leaned in. "He's playing you."

"Yeah, I know." Again, nothing new there.

"No, I mean, that's what he said. That he's playing you and expecting to get a big paycheck out of it. The other guy told him that no one would believe a loser like him. But Ralph said it didn't matter because he'd get his payoff before y'all even went to court."

What did this mean? Could they use this information somehow? But it'd only be the word of a bartender against that of the felon.

"I just wanted you to know." She took a sip of her water. "You and that ministry of yours do a lot of good. No one wants to see you get taken to the cleaners like this, especially not for some loser drunk like Ralph Emmerson."

"Would you be willing to testify to all this?"

"I can do one better." She placed her phone on the table and tapped the screen. "I recorded everything. Sent it to myself using a voice-recording app."

He blinked. Could it really be that easy? *Lord, this is You, isn't it?* It had to be. This whole scenario was too perfect not to be God-orchestrated. He released a breath, so relieved he nearly laughed. "Can you forward that to me? And my lawyer, too?"

"Um...maybe. Let me see if I can find you." She tapped on her phone a few times. Then it responded with a *whoosh*. She grinned. "Sent."

It took all his self-control not to jump up with a whoop, but the grin expanding across his face likely conveyed his enthusiasm. "Thank you, Amanda. I cannot thank you enough for this. Really."

"No problem. If you need anything else, don't be afraid to holler. You got my number now, and know where to find me on social media." She laughed.

"I will." Noah's lawyer might want her to testify, though he doubted it'd get that far. Once Ralph heard his slurred voice touting trash in that recording, he'd drop his lawsuit right quick.

Noah returned home to find Kayla sitting on the front steps while Timber kicked a large ball around. When Timber saw him, he squealed, "Unca!" and came running toward him.

Noah picked him up, tossed him over his shoulder, then dropped him back to his feet. It felt good to have someone so excited to see him. "Hey, bud. You been good for Aunt Kayla?"

He nodded and toddled back toward his ball. She stood and dusted off her hands. "You seem chipper. Good meeting?"

He grinned. "Better than good." He relayed what the bartender had told him.

"Is that legal? To record a conversation without a person's knowledge?"

He frowned. "As far as I know." *Please don't tell me that woman's recording, today's meeting, was all for nothing.* Just when his hopes had started to rise again. "Worst-case scenario, she can testify to what she heard. But at least now my lawyer's got something concrete to work with." And if nothing else, today's encounter reminded him that God was with him and his ministry. When life became crazy, it was easy to forget that.

He glanced past her, through the opened door of the house. "How's Sophia?"

"Probably dreaming about a river of formula and mashed bananas."

"Appetizing. No more fussing?"

She shook her head. "Been happy as a baby in a satin blanket ever since our walk yesterday."

He studied her. "What's up? I can tell you've got a lot of thoughts swirling, fighting to come out."

"I came to Sage Creek to make sure the kids were okay. I never expected to fall in love."

With him?

"But those children…"

His heart sank. Of course, she'd been talking about them.

"I know I've never been a mom." Tears shone in her eyes. "So I can't really say this, but I love them as if they were my own. You know?"

He swallowed. "And you and I, do we have a chance?" The question he'd been aching to ask had finally popped out. Only now he wished he could take it back, because in the not knowing, at least there was hope. But if she turned him down? He wasn't sure he could take that.

"Honest answer?"

He winced inwardly but kept his expression blank. "Yeah."

"I don't know. I care about you. I really do. Under different circumstances, maybe." She sighed. "But everything feels so complicated, not to mention our worlds are so far apart."

"Think you might move here?" *For me?*

She studied him for a moment, and tiny lines were etched across her forehead. "What about my business? I built it from scratch. Poured my heart and soul into it for nearly ten years."

"Your assistant seems to be managing it well enough."

She gave a defeated laugh. "I'm not so sure about

that. Besides, interior designing is who I am. I can't give
that up."

"Start something here. Remodeling businesses, man
caves and nurseries."

"What about you? Can you see yourself living in the
Pacific Northwest?"

Could he, for her? His ministry was doing a world of
good for so many. Men were getting their lives—and their
families—back. Legacies were being changed. Could
Helping Hands survive without him? And how would
he earn a living? He'd promised his mom he'd never return to bull-riding.

Inside, Sophia started to cry. He turned toward the
house. "Coming, baby girl." He paused just inside to
glance back. "Can we finish this talk later?" Though he
really didn't want to. He wanted to deal with it all now,
to know where they stood and if there was any hope for
the two of them.

"Sure. I should go, anyway."

How had he grown so attached to all three of them in
such a short period of time?

Chapter Eighteen

Sunday after church, with Noah's dad spending the morning at the senior center, his mom had asked to take the kids for a while. That left him with too much time on his hands to think—or worry himself into a hole, as his mom liked to call it. He figured mucking out a few stalls would occupy his mind enough.

"Bro."

He glanced up to see Elliot coming toward him. "Hey."

"Figured I'd find you out here." Elliot studied him for a minute. "You look like you done lost your best friend."

"Guess I've had a good day and bad. S'pose I should be focusing on the good, instead of all the what-ifs." Noah told him the latest details. "Regardless, seems clear to me Kayla isn't going to stick around long. And with how much she loves those kids…" His throat felt scratchy. "I worry I might lose all of them."

"So change her mind."

"What do you mean?"

"What are you doing to snag her for good? Capture her heart, sure and proper. 'Cause having her watch your kids? That's not romantic, bro."

"I already took her out." He told him about their night at the dinner theater, and the ice cream after.

"And she knew that was a date? Because seems to me, the way you tell it, that was just two friends helping the other friend out, and tending to their sweet tooth after."

"You come in here to bug me for a reason?"

"Besides solving all your relationship woes?" He chuckled. "Yeah. Met a guy from the Fellowship for Christian Bikers club. He wanted to know what we do, and I suggested he invite you to come speak to him and his group. Figured maybe they'd be interested in helping us financially."

"When?"

"He didn't say."

"Have him call me." Men in those types of groups often became some of their biggest donors. Guys who'd been where the men Helping Hands served were grateful to have climbed out, and were looking to give back.

"Cool. Guess I better leave you to plot your first date with that cute little filly of yours."

First date. An odd jolt, similar to how he felt in high school, whenever the teacher called on him, swept through him.

He wasn't exactly a dating pro. During his rodeo days, drinking had always dulled his jitters…and his common sense. Since then, he'd hardly been a ladies' man. The last woman he'd taken out, other than Kayla, spent the entire evening talking about her ex-boyfriend. Prior to that, he'd surprised a sweet gal from church with a picnic, only to end up caught in a rainstorm. Their hike back to his truck had been a swampy, muddy mess.

If he really wanted to capture Kayla's heart, he'd need something more special than Wilma's Café, something memorable. But what?

He returned his shovel to its hook, set out some clean straw in each of the stalls, then headed inside. The office was quiet and the scent of stale coffee hung in the air.

His office was a mess, as he'd left it. Invoices piled on the corner of his desk next to a jumble of notes.

Noah sat behind his computer and jiggled the mouse to wake up his screen. He typed "summer activities" in his browser. Geocaching? Nah. Foraging? Had someone really listed that? He scrolled down, stopped. Lavender, her favorite flower. He could take her to a lavender farm in Houston.

He grabbed his phone and tapped her number before his courage failed.

"Noah, hi. Is everything okay?"

"Yeah. I was just… I was wondering if… What I mean to say is…" He took a deep breath and released it slowly. "You busy tonight?"

"Tonight?"

"Yeah. I'd like to pick you up, like around four, if that works."

"For what?"

"It's a surprise. But maybe dress cute." Heat shot up his neck. "I mean, you always look great, but, like, not really Sunday morning. Maybe one of your sundresses or something. Or whatever. You can wear whatever."

Silence followed, and his gut clenched. She was going to say no. She'd picked up on his intent and wasn't interested. Hadn't she made it clear she'd come to Sage Creek for the kids?

He rubbed his forehead. "You know what? I shouldn't have—"

"I'd love to."

He exhaled. "What?"

"I'd love to."

Kayla scrutinized her reflection in the beauty-salon mirror. "I hate to be your most boring client of the day, but I just want a trim and my highlights touched up some."

Trista fluffed Kayla's hair, stepped back with her head tilted, then fluffed it again. "You sure? Because with your skin tone, a hint of blue would look amazing."

She laughed. "Unfortunately, I'm not that brave."

"Noah would love it and you know it."

Kayla's face heated at the mention of his name.

Trista jerked back with her hand to her chest. "Girl. You've got it bad."

Kayla wanted to crawl under the salon chair. She was certain everyone else in the salon—not to mention all the men in the barbershop sharing the other half of the retail space—was staring at her. "What are you talking about?"

"Noah Williams. You've fallen hard for him, haven't you?" She shook her head with a knowing smile. "This is serious. Like put-your-condo-on-the-market-and-move-to-Sage-Creek-tomorrow serious."

"Hardly."

"Give me one good reason why not."

"For starters, I need to earn a living."

"Redesign my salon."

Kayla rolled her eyes. "You don't have the money to fund my love life—even if it were worth the expense."

"As to your charity implication, that's hardly what this is. I've done told you half a dozen times, this place is long overdue for a remodel. You'd be doing me a favor."

She turned Kayla's chair to face her head-on. "I'd hate to see you lose a really good thing with Noah." She dropped her comb on the counter. "Come on. Let's get your hair washed."

Kayla followed her to a small alcove with three sinks positioned side by side, then leaned back as warm water flowed over her scalp. "Mmm. That feels so good. I didn't realize how tense I was."

"Not surprised, carrying the world on your shoulders

like you are." Trista wrapped a towel around Kayla's head then guided her to her feet. "Really makes me angry, all this pain your sister caused. Leaving a baby unattended in a house full of liquor but no food. And don't even get me started on their good-for-nothing, baby-leaving daddy." She sighed. "Sorry. I don't mean to be so snarky. Like I said, I'm just angry."

Kayla was, too. And sad. And confused.

Trista ran her comb through Kayla's damp hair. "But I suspect my anger isn't helping you none. So, how about you draw up some plans for bringing my salon into the twenty-first century?" She glanced toward Henry Shedd, the barber occupying the adjacent space. "What do you think, Henry?" He and Trista shared the space, probably to keep rent manageable. His barbershop stood on one side of the large area, her salon on the other, a half-dividing wall between them. "Want Kayla to give your place a makeover? She'll be doing mine."

Henry grunted and returned to shaving a man's head.

Kayla frowned. "I never agreed—"

"Pshaw." Trista flicked a hand. "You will. Now…" She spritzed Kayla's hair with hair spray. "Tell me what Romeo has planned for his Cinderella tonight."

Kayla rolled her eyes. "Must you make everything so dramatic? And I have no idea."

"Oooh! A surprise. Love it."

Kayla had to admit, she did, too. Noah Williams, former rough and burly bull rider, sure could be romantic when he wanted to be.

If only their lives had intertwined earlier, before this whole Christy mess.

Chapter Nineteen

Noah met Kayla at her hotel, reached his truck before her and opened the door for her. Her hair looked different somehow. More highlights, maybe? The auburn streaks were more pronounced, which brought out the pink undertones in her skin.

"You look nice."

A soft blush lit her cheeks, and she dropped her gaze. "Thanks."

He closed her door, then got in on the driver's side. Hopefully the rain would hold off, but the way those dark clouds hovered on the horizon, he wasn't so sure. Of all the days for a storm to hit, did it have to be when he'd planned an outdoor excursion with the woman he…?

Did he love her? Was that what he was feeling? Why he couldn't get her out of his mind and his heart hurt whenever he thought of her leaving?

"Any chance you'll tell me where we're going yet?" Kayla fastened her seat belt as Noah pulled out onto the county road.

He grinned. "Nope."

"Somewhere in town?"

He meandered through a residential area. "Hmm…"

"Indoors or outdoors?"

"Such great questions." The skin crinkled around his eyes.

"Can you at least tell me if I'll need sunscreen?"

"Nice try."

She huffed, but the upturned corners of her mouth belied her mock frustration.

By the time they reached the two-lane highway heading out of town, her questions regarding their eventual location shifted. "How long have you been running Helping Hands?"

He gazed toward the road ahead, mentally counting backward. "Going on eight, nine years, give or take."

"Do you ever wonder why some people get better, and others, like my sister and your brother, don't?"

"All the time. I can't say I have an answer, except God's got to get a hold of their heart. They have to want to change. And I guess they have to hit a place where they feel where they're at is harder, more painful, than whatever it'll take to change. Then there's the whole physiological aspect of addiction."

"I keep trying to go back, to pinpoint when things first went wrong with Christy. I mean, I get her grief regarding our parents, and her anger that followed. I felt that, too. Maybe not as intensely, but every holiday, every Mother's Day or Father's Day, was a reminder that we were basically orphans. Our grandparents tried so hard to give us a normal life, to compensate for all we'd lost."

"I suspect nothing can ever truly compensate for the loss of a loved one."

"True." She sighed. "And now I feel like I'm losing another one. Like I'm mourning my sister. And it almost feels harder than when I grieved our parents. Because there's no closure."

He placed his hand on hers. "I get it." For years, his emotions regarding JD's addiction and self-destruction felt like a Texas spring—filled with hope one day, then pummeled with hail the next. Just when Noah had resolved himself to the fact that his brother wasn't going to get any better, JD would start coming around again talking about going to rehab, only to disappear a few days later.

"I wish I could tell you this gets easier over time," he said. "All's I can say is God sees your pain, and He'll hold you through it, if you let Him."

Just outside of Houston, he followed his GPS down a long dirt road lined with trees. A field, backing up to rolling hills, stood behind a split-rail fence. The lilacs must still be around the bend. He cast Kayla a sideways glance, anxious to see the look in her eyes when she realized where he'd brought her.

Assuming she really did like lavender as much as he thought.

Enough to drive an hour away and spend the day at a flower farm?

What if his brilliant idea turned into a dud?

The road curved right, then forked. A sign with a painted floral border said Hill Country Lavender Farm.

"What's this?" Kayla asked.

He shrugged. "Figured you might enjoy coming out here, with your love of lavender and all. They've got live music, a little market and… Well, you'll see."

"But how did you…? Noah, you're something else. You know that?"

"Just keep thinking that." He made a mental fist pump. Score one for his Impress Kayla campaign.

"But…are they still open? It's after five."

"You'll see." He followed a dirt road between two lavender fields in full bloom to a gravel lot positioned in front of a yellow farmhouse with white trim and a pale green door. Lavender grew from large pots flanking the stairs, and on the covered porch a small metal table centered two white rockers.

The scent of yeasty vanilla and something else sweet he couldn't place swept over him as they stepped out of his truck, and the acoustics of a bluegrass melody carried on the air.

Shielding her eyes from the sun, she gazed toward a faded brown barn with a metal roof to the vast purple fields beyond.

He came alongside her and gave her waist a squeeze. "You hungry?"

"Actually, I am."

Her smile warmed him from his toes up.

He grinned. "Good."

She grabbed on to his hand with hers and hugged his forearm to her. "Thanks for this."

"Anything for you." He meant it. He'd give her the world, if he could. "Give me a second." Reluctantly releasing her, he dashed into the entrance. A woman wearing a bonnet and an old Western dress with a ruffled apron stood in front of a counter adorned with various lavender-infused products.

"Welcome to Hill Country Lavender Farm." She smiled. "Are you here for a self-guided tour, the festival or one of our scheduled activities?"

"I paid for dinner for two beneath the oak."

"Lovely." She grabbed a pamphlet and opened it to a map. "You'll want to follow the sweet Bandera trail through our east fields. It'll curve around, past the Rosenbauch Garden to Hidden Cove. We've got your table all set up for you." She rounded the counter, produced a notebook from beneath it and flipped it open. "What did you say your name was?"

"Noah Williams."

"Yep. Got you down for dinner for two." She handed him two purple tickets adorned with lavender sprigs.

"Thanks." Tickets in hand, he bounded outside to find Kayla shooting close-up pictures of a butterfly resting on one of the potted flowers. He placed a hand to her back. "You ready?"

She startled, then smiled. "Absolutely."

Taking her hand, he guided her past bundles of lavender laid across a long wooden table to the path dissecting the wind-rustling fields. A minty, almost smoky scent wafted over them.

She turned pensive.

"You seem deep in thought," he said.

"After my parents died, my sister and I went to live with our grandparents in Houston," she said. "That was a hard move, to leave my friends, the town we'd grown up in, our faith community."

"I imagine."

"Plus, I was pretty depressed. I pulled into myself, didn't really talk to anyone. As you can imagine, I didn't have a whole lot of friends. Actually, I had none." She gave a sighed laugh. "That first summer, I took a job watching a lady's kids. She was widowed. Her husband died in a hunting accident. He left her with an old, broken-down house, a lot of land and not much else. Plus three rambunctious kids who were likely dealing with their own grief."

"I read something about that—that kids can act out when they're sad." He'd often wondered if that was the cause of some of Timber's temper tantrums and fighting bedtime.

They rounded a corner. Lavender fields extended to

their left and a thick cluster of trees stretched in front of them.

She picked up a twig and snapped off its tiny branches. "I didn't like being home, at my grandparents'. They tried, but maybe they tried too hard, you know? Seemed they were always pestering me to talk about my parents' deaths. Plus, my sister started rebelling. She was always yelling, getting angry over every little thing. And then she started drinking. Maybe I should've helped her." She sniffed. "But I didn't. I just left, whenever I could. I stayed over at Irene's—that was the woman's name. Sometimes for a week at a time."

"I'm sorry."

She stopped and gazed toward the green-and-purple hilltops in the distance. "Her property backed to an orchard with tufts of wild lavender. It always felt so peaceful, so far away from everyone. I'd stay there for hours. And God met me there. I didn't hear an audible voice or anything like that, but I just knew He was there. With me."

Had bringing her here triggered painful memories? He came to her side and took her hands in his. "That's why you love the flowers so much, huh?"

"Maybe so."

His gaze dropped to her mouth. What would it be like to kiss those soft lips? To hold her close? To spend his mornings sipping coffee with this beautiful creature, hear about her plans, her hurts and her dreams? To be entrusted with her heart?

With a deep breath, she pulled away and glanced about. "Which way now?"

In other words, back off. He fought a sigh. The path in front of them forked, one way winding through more lavender fields, likely looping back to the farmhouse, the other to the trees.

"This way." Hand to her back, he guided her through the trees to a cluster of tables covered with white linen and purple runners. Lavender sprigs in mason jars adorned with lace centered the tables, and tulle decorated the white folding chairs.

"Noah." She stopped, hand to her chest. When she turned toward him, the look of adoration, of—of...love? It just about buckled his knees. "This is beautiful."

"Welcome." A woman dressed similar to the gal at the farmhouse greeted them and led them to a table for two. "Would you care for a glass of lavender lemonade?"

He held out Kayla's chair for her. "That'd be great, thanks."

Others, primarily couples and two young families with girls wearing ruffled dresses, joined them. But Noah hardly noticed them. His focus zeroed in on the captivating woman sitting across from him. She spoke of her business, of her love for scrapbooking—who knew? And mostly, of all the hilarious and cute things Timber and Sophia did while he was at work. And for a moment, he let himself imagine what it might be like to be married to this woman, for the four of them to form a family.

If only he could convince her to stay.

For the next couple of hours, they ate a variety of foods that one might see on the cover of magazines. Appetizers that looked too pretty to eat, salad with weed-looking leaves and candied nuts, pork medallions. They finished their meal with white cookies drizzled in almond icing and garnished with dried lavender.

Kayla took a sip of her drink. "This has been amazing. Thank you."

Music played from somewhere behind them, and midway through the second song, one of the couples stood and ambled to a grassy area beneath the branches of a towering oak. Soon, another couple joined them.

"Will you do me the honor?" He held out his hand, and she placed hers, soft and featherlight, in his. Her shy smile returned as she let him lead her onto the makeshift "dance floor."

At first their steps were formal, almost as if she felt self-conscious. But by the next song, she leaned in closer and rested her cheek on his chest. He closed his eyes, arm circled around her back, and breathed in her sweet strawberry-jasmine scent.

Giggles drew his attention to a family on his left. A dad and very pregnant mom were dancing with a wiggly, giggly little one who looked maybe eighteen months old sandwiched between them. The dad whispered something to the mom, and she laughed. Then he kissed her cheek, then his daughter's, before spinning them both around.

Noah turned his attention back to Kayla, who was still watching the family. He cupped her chin in his hand and tilted her face so that her gaze met his. "That could be us, you know."

Her eyes searched his, and her mouth parted slightly as if she wanted to say something. But then she leaned her cheek on his chest, letting him hold her for the remainder of the dance.

And for now, that was enough.

Chapter Twenty

The next morning, Kayla took extra time getting ready. She tried on three different outfits and fiddled with her hair so much it turned flyaway and she had to spritz it and start again.

She was acting ridiculous. She'd had one night of dancing. Okay, two. Two nights of dancing with Noah, and she was acting like a silly schoolgirl with her first crush. For a day of being a nanny, no less.

Being a nanny for perhaps the kindest, most thoughtful man she'd ever met. She closed her eyes, remembering the sound of his steady heartbeat beneath her ear, as he led her around the dance area.

That could be us, you know. His voice had been low, deep, yet almost pleading.

In that moment, it'd taken every ounce of self-control she had not to accept his veiled invitation.

What would happen if she gave in? If she followed her heart and held tight to this man who had managed to two-step his way into her life?

Would she have to give up her business?

She huffed, snapped her blush compact closed and marched into the kitchen to refill her coffee mug. Her cell phone chimed, followed by the automatic-caller announcement. The county jail? That had to be a crank call. She started to hit Decline, but, curious, pressed Answer instead.

"Hello?"

"Kayla?" Christy's voice trembled. "I'm in big trouble."

Her hand tightened around her phone. "Where are you? What happened?"

"I was at a party with some friends and—"

"You got pulled over for a DUI. Again." Kayla closed her eyes and pinched the bridge of her nose. "I'm not bailing you—"

"I got in an accident. I didn't mean to. I know I shouldn't have been driving, but the party got boring, so I took off." Her words tumbled out, but then she paused. "Kayla? I killed a man." She gave a hiccuped sob. "A father. I don't know what happened to his wife and daughter. The ambulance rushed them to the hospital."

No. Please, no. Not this.

"Kayla? What do I do?"

This couldn't be real. Christy could be facing serious charges. A possible life sentence. And that poor family. "How old?"

"What?"

"The child. How old is she?"

Christy didn't respond right away, and when she did, her voice sounded small. "I don't know."

Tears sprang to Kayla's eyes as an image of a precious little girl, lying on a stretcher, came to mind. Someone else's Timber. *Oh, dear Jesus, how did this happen?*

"Kayla, please. I need a lawyer. And a bondsman. You have to help me. I don't know who else to call, and I'm broke."

This was going to destroy their grandparents. Whether

or not Christy beat the charges—did Kayla even want her to? "Maybe jail is the best place for you right now." She spoke softly, her throat tight and scratchy.

"How can you say that? I didn't mean for this to happen!"

"You chose to drink. You chose to drive, and the moment you sat behind that wheel, you chose to put every life you came into contact with in danger."

"Don't you dare judge me."

A father dead. A mother and child hospitalized, maybe fighting for their last breath at this moment.

"I've got to go."

"No, pl—"

She ended the call, let her phone drop and sat, staring at the wall in front of her.

At Kayla's soft knock, Noah answered his door to find her standing, shoulders slumped, on his stoop. She looked as if the life had been drained from her. "You okay?"

Her eyes searched his for a moment, but then she stepped inside and headed straight for the couch. She sat with elbows on her knees, hands clasped between them, gaze on the floor.

"Aunt Kay-kay!" Still dressed in his pj's and with his hair sticking every which way, Timber toddled toward her and practically flung himself in her lap.

She wrapped an arm around him and pulled him close. "Hey, bud." Her voice sounded flat. She rested her chin on his head.

"Hey." Noah sat beside her and placed a hand on her back. "What's going on, Kayla?"

Moisture pooled in her eyes. "Christy's in jail." The story she then told him twisted his gut.

"What if the mom and little girl don't make it? Now what, Noah? Now what?"

"I wish I knew." There was no way he was going in to work this morning. Meetings or not, Kayla needed him, and he intended to be here for her. "Come here."

She gave a sniffled sob and wrapped her arms around him in a tight hug, little Timber sandwiched between them.

"Don't you have an important meeting with that missions organization from Austin this morning?" Kayla asked. "To give them a tour of your facility or something?"

He thumbed away her tears. "Elliot can handle it." And if the fellas driving in had a problem with his absence, then maybe Helping Hands didn't need their donations after all. One thing Noah had promised himself long ago—he'd never allow the ministry to crowd out his most important relationships. After all, a man couldn't teach others how to love their families and friends like Jesus if he wasn't doing the same.

He cupped Kayla's chin in his hands. "Everything will work out." He kissed her forehead. "Promise."

Christy's social worker called about twenty minutes later. Apparently news hit her office fast. Should he answer with Kayla sitting beside him? He cast a glance her way and tapped his screen. "Hey, can I call you back?"

"Is Kayla with you?"

"Yeah."

"She should probably hear this, too. It's about the kids and their mom."

Jaw firm, Kayla motioned for him to continue, as if she knew who'd called and why. Though hesitant, he nodded and put the call on speaker. "We're both here."

"Good morning." After some gentle apologies, the social worker told them what they already knew. "Christy's facing vehicular manslaughter and two counts of vehicular assault—assuming mom and daughter pull through, which is iffy right now—and her third DUI."

"How much jail time will she get, do you think?" Kayla's tense yet wounded expression made him wish he'd kept the call between him and the social worker. But they needed to be able to talk openly about stuff like this, as painful as this might be.

"Anywhere from two to twenty years with fines up to ten thousand dollars. Considering her history, the combination of charges and the fact that the accident occurred in Judge Mason's territory, I wouldn't be surprised if she got ten to fifteen."

"What would that mean for Timber and Sophia?"

"She could lose her parental rights. The state doesn't like to keep kids in the system long. Wants them reunited with their parents or adopted."

He swallowed, his stomach queasy. "Would they be able to stay with me?"

"That's the plan for now." As usual, she answered his question like a politician. But she probably had to remain vague, legally speaking, until things were set in legal ink. "They're doing very well, and you're doing a great job with them."

He wanted to whoop, but deep sorrow tinged his celebration—the ache of knowing a family had been shattered, a young life destroyed and two little ones quite likely would lose their mother.

When the call ended, he glanced at Kayla once again. She was staring at her hands. The quick blinking of her eyes suggested she was fighting back tears.

He placed his arm over her shoulder. "I'm sorry."

With a deep breath, Kayla pulled her phone from her purse. "If you'll excuse me, I need to call my assistant. Let her know I'll be staying in Texas longer than expected."

Chapter Twenty-One

The next morning, Kayla took the children to the library for a special toddler craft activity. But first she stopped by the Literary Sweet Spot for some treats.

Timber bolted toward a display of chocolates, but Kayla snagged him by the wrist. "Sorry, bud. How about you help me pick out snacks for your party instead." She steered him and the stroller to the counter, where Leslie stood wearing a bright floral apron. Her long blond hair was in its usual messy bun. Flour dusted her cheek.

"Hi."

"Good to see you." Her intense yet kind gaze made Kayla tense and suggested word had gotten out about her sister's arrest. Of course it would. A death so close to home had probably made the front page of their newspaper.

Leslie smoothed wayward bangs off her forehead with the back of her hand. "You hungry or just looking for your regular caffeine fix?"

Kayla released a breath and smiled, grateful her friend hadn't pried or brought attention to her family's tragedy. "Both, along with two dozen sugar cookies." She eyed the display counter, filled with everything from truffles to double-fudge brownies.

"I don't have that many, sorry. But I could do a mix-and-match, if you're okay with that."

"Sure. Whatever you give me will be happily eaten, I'm sure. It's my turn to bring snacks."

"Me one?" Timber pressed his nose and two chubby hands to the dessert case.

"Sorry." Kayla offered Leslie a sheepish smile, then tugged him to her side. "In a bit, bud."

"No worries." Leslie waved a hand and began loading baked goods into a shallow cake box. The scents of cinnamon and vanilla wafted up. "By the way, I've decided to give myself—well, my business—a birthday gift this year."

"Oh?"

"A children's area, like you see in those fancy, big-city bookstores. I already talked to Drake, Faith's husband. He said he'd cut me a deal on the remodel. I'd love a legit tree house with a reading nook. Maybe some animal-shaped beanbags. What do you think?"

"Sounds lovely."

"Think you can help? I'd pay, of course. And no rush. Whenever you finish with the hair salon."

"Ah. So, Trista's been by, has she?"

"Every Tuesday and Thursday afternoon, like clockwork."

"And just how many people did she tell about her potential remodel?" One Kayla didn't remember committing to. She was about to say she didn't have time, that she needed to get back to her business in Washington as soon as possible. But thanks to Christy's accident, she'd be sticking around for who knew how long.

Maybe even for good? Her heart skipped as an image of Noah's gentle eyes came to mind.

Leslie closed the dessert box and rang up the order.

"You know how she likes to talk once she gets excited about something."

"That I do." And though neither project promised the payout or prestige as her Whidbey Island clients would, it felt good to be appreciated. These were her people. Somehow she'd forgotten that.

What if she stayed? To help Noah raise the kids and forge a life with him? With all three of them? Her grandparents would be ecstatic. Clients here likely couldn't pay nearly as much as those on the West Coast, but the cost of living would be less, and she wouldn't have to rely completely on herself. She'd have Noah.

It felt good to say that.

But was that what he wanted? Not just help with the kids, not just a dancing partner, but a lifelong companion? Someone to hold tight to, through the silly and the hard? Someone to grow old with?

Leslie gave Kayla her change. "So what do you say? Think you can help me out with my amazing, adorable, giggle-and-memory-producing ideas?"

She smiled. "I'll get a proposal to you by week's end." She tucked the dessert box in the basket of Sophia's stroller, grabbed Timber's chubby little hand and maneuvered her way out onto the sidewalk. The sun was out, the temperature warm but pleasant and the library but a few blocks down. No reason to wrangle Timber back into his car seat.

Across the way, Lucy and Doris exited Wilma's, arm in arm. Those two were almost as adorable as the toddlers she was about to encounter. It warmed her heart, the way the younger woman had taken to watching over Doris. Back when Kayla was in school, their roles had been reversed, as Doris had once mentored Lucy. They reminded Kayla of just how deep relationships in this small, quiet town ran. Sage Creek might not have a lot of fancy restaurants or museums or multilevel shopping malls, but it promised the sense of belonging she'd been missing.

She had time to kill, so she popped into a store with a train table and hand-carved locomotives. She listened to Mr. and Mrs. Schmidt, the store owners, share stories of their grandchildren while Timber played and Sophia drifted in and out of sleep. By the time she made it to the library some twenty minutes later, she'd finished her latte and Sophia had fallen asleep.

The other toddlers and their moms trickled in slowly. While the librarian led the children in some simple games, Kayla flipped through some parenting magazines someone had left on a nearby table. She turned to a caterpillar treat made from celery sticks, raisins and candy. Timber would love those. The next page provided tips for dealing with toddler tantrums.

"Now, there's an article I need to copy and frame."

She startled at the sound of Noah's voice, then smiled. "Hi. What're you doing here?"

"My morning meeting got canceled. Figured I'd join you and little man for a spell."

He glanced back at the magazine. "The art of redirecting. I could've used those tips last night."

"Why do you say that?"

"Timber was wound up something awful last night, peppering me with the same question over and over."

"About?"

"Junk food. I made the mistake of telling him you and he were bringing the snack, started tossing out random ideas of what you might bring. Guess I made the little guy hungry."

"So you ran in town for something sweet?"

"Hey now." He crossed his arms with a look of mocked

offense. "What kind of uncle do you think I am? One who can't tell his favorite nephew *no*?"

She raised an eyebrow.

He laughed. "I popped over to Brenda's. She keeps enough baking supplies on hand to stock the Literary Sweet Spot."

She shook her head. "You're a mess. But you know what they say—" She flipped to the article she'd just skimmed. "If you can't tell them *no* when they're toddlers, you'll really struggle once they hit the teen years."

"It says that?"

Nodding, she rotated the page so he could better see it.

"Reckon the only answer, then, is for you to help me." His gaze intensified.

She swallowed. "What do you mean?"

"I'd like you to stay. Here in Sage Creek. Timber and Sophia need you. I need you. I've never fathered kids before and didn't have the best role model. Least, not until Ben came around. Plus, you're great with them. They've grown to love you."

Her heart wanted to say yes. What if she did? What if she took the leap, let Nicole manage the business in Washington and launched a sister firm here?

She took a deep breath and smoothed her hair off her forehead. "I'm touched by your words. I love those kids as if they were my own, but I've got a lot to consider." She needed to talk with Nicole. "What I can tell you is I'm here for now."

"Okay." He remained silent after that, and it tore her heart to see the sadness in his eyes. To know that she was the cause.

Her phone dinged, and she glanced at the screen. She recognized the area code but not the number. "Kayla Fisher, Fresh Look Interiors. May I help you?"

"Yes, hello. My name is Raymond Hawley. I own the Ocean Front Cabin, a bed-and-breakfast in La Conner. I just purchased the property, actually, and am looking for design help. I was told you had an eye for rustic-chic."

"Absolutely. What were you thinking?"

"A friend of mine—he owns Odds and Ends in north Seattle—showed me some promotional material you sent him, and I really liked it."

"Are you referring to the furnishings created by Helping Hands."

"Right. The chairs would look great on our covered-porch area and our back patio. Are they outdoor-compatible?"

"They can be made so, yes." She reached into her purse and took out her pocket notebook. "How many chairs were you looking for?"

"Four up front, maybe… Three table sets, all seating four, for the back. I'd also love a large table for twelve to fourteen, with bench seating on one side and chairs for the rest. Is that possible?"

"Can you hold, please?" She put her phone on Mute and relayed the conversation to Noah. "This is huge. Not just in terms of immediate sales, but it could break you into the Northwest, and who knows where else, considering all the tourists this guy will likely see."

"The chairs and four-top tables won't be a problem, but his dining set might take some time. When's he hoping to open?"

She returned to her call and repeated Noah's question.

"When's the soonest you can deliver?"

"How about if I take down your information and send you a formal proposal, along with an estimated cost and timeline?"

"That'll work."

She asked him a few more questions, got color and

tone preferences, room dimensions and numbers. Then, while Timber enjoyed story time and Sophia took her midmorning nap, she and Noah talked it all out.

Noah ran the back of his hand beneath his beard. "Honestly, the sooner we can do this, the better. We need the money. And I've got some talented buddies willing to work for free so long as we feed them."

"So, what? A month?"

"Two weeks."

"Really?"

"Yep. Let's do this."

She grinned. "All right, partner." It felt good to say that, to think that maybe the two of them could work together after all. Maybe this was God's way of moving Noah and the kids to Washington State.

Later that afternoon, Kayla texted Nicole requesting a video meeting.

They connected during naptime. "Hey, Nicole. Thanks for taking the time to chat with me today."

"For sure. Is everything all right?"

"I wanted to talk more about my stay. About me staying in Texas longer than I anticipated. Would that be overly challenging? I know you've likely been working a lot more hours than normal."

"That won't be a problem. I've got everything handled. You do what you need to do."

Kayla chose to believe her, and even if she didn't, there really wasn't much else she could do. She simply couldn't return to Washington yet. "You deserve a raise."

"Really? Can you afford that? Not to sound rude, but I know traveling can be expensive, and business is always a bit slower during the winter."

"You deserve it. And besides, after this week, I'll be staying with a friend, which means no more hotel fees."

She didn't have a lot of funds to spare, but Nicole had taken on a great deal more responsibility. Plus, they had a lot of prospects that, if they handled them right, could set them up great for what was likely to be a slow winter. "I appreciate how hard you're working." And though she'd made some mistakes—some big mistakes—at least she was teachable. Sometimes a person learned most through their blunders. "Your willingness to step up in my absence."

"We're a team."

"Exactly."

"I got a call for an interview from a design firm in Chicago."

"Oh?" Her gut swirled. *Not now.*

"I told them I'd changed my mind. I mean, I want to progress as a designer, obviously, but I guess I don't need to forge my own way anymore."

"Why is that?"

"I feel like more than just an employee now. Like I'm a vital part of Fresh Look Interiors."

"You didn't before?"

"I knew I was helpful, made things easier or whatever, but honestly, you could've handled everything."

"I'm sorry. I didn't realize."

"What I'm trying to say is that it's been nice to be needed."

"You are. Very much so." They said their goodbyes and she slipped her phone into her purse.

So Kayla being in Sage Creek had been a good thing. Perhaps even saved the best employee she'd ever had. Maybe what the Bible said about God turning all things to good was true, and if so, He'd do the same in regard to Noah, Timber, Sophia and Christy. And if Christy was convicted?

Maybe going to jail could help her conquer her addictions. Then Kayla could get her sister back.

She smiled, remembering the morning she, Noah and the kids had walked to the stables. The sun had been out, but a steady yet gentle breeze kept the temperature pleasant. Timber had been so adorable, bouncing around, as had Sophia, with all her cooing and babbling. The sense of peace and security she'd felt when Noah placed his arm around her and promised to protect her and the kids.

Because she'd been concerned, having seen the rough men his ministry served hanging about the place. Men with sketchy backgrounds, trying to beat drugs and alcohol, just like Christy.

Kayla was beginning to understand what a difficult road that was, and how drugs could change a person. She crossed the room to the window, then peeked out toward Helping Hands. As usual, a handful of vehicles, all older and dented or rusted—or both—filled the lot. She wanted to believe Noah's assurances regarding those men, about the kids living but a stone's throw away from the facility. But drug addicts were about as predictable as a Texas storm brewing on the horizon. Could shift right, could dissipate entirely, or could turn into the worst tornado the county had seen in twenty years.

And yet, though his ministry concerned her, it also drew her to him. His love for others, and for the kids, was so evident. He was gentle, kind, strong, a man of integrity.

The kind of man any woman would be lucky to have for a husband.

Chapter Twenty-Two

While Noah waited in line at the hardware store, he scanned his neglected email inbox. Mr. Crawford, a local businessman, had sent him a message asking to meet.

He checked his calendar, accepted the invite, then shot Elliot and Brenda a text letting them know of his change of plans. He'd been hoping to catch up on paperwork and phone calls today, anyway. No reason he couldn't push those things out to Monday.

He arrived at Wilma's ten minutes early and sipped coffee while he waited. Sally Jo strolled over with a damp rag in hand and two menus tucked under her arm. "You win the lottery or something?"

He furrowed his brow. "What?"

"Seems you can barely keep from grinning."

He laughed. "God's been good, is all." At least, it seemed that way. Though there was no guarantee that man from La Conner would accept their proposal. Still, things were looking up. His lawyer expected Ralph to drop his lawsuit, and though Noah would still be out most of his retainer, they could bounce back from that. Especially if he sold all those furniture pieces that bed-and-breakfast owner was asking for.

And he and Kayla were working together. That meant something, right?

Maybe they could do the same closer to home, target bed-and-breakfasts along the Gulf Coast, and Helping Hands could expand to other pieces, like maybe those bookshelves that looked like boats.

That wouldn't be hard at all. Even his newbies could manage that.

Could be that Ralph's lawsuit, as much as it'd hurt initially, had actually initiated something good in getting Noah to take Helping Hands national. He'd been talking about doing that for a long time, but had never put anything more than thought into it, mainly because he felt too busy. But that'd always be the case. If this scenario taught him anything, it was not to spend so much time chasing a thousand little fires that he neglected what was really important.

Mr. Crawford entered wearing slacks and a button-down shirt. He saw Noah and, with a brisk nod, strode over. Noah stood to shake his hand.

"Thanks for coming," Mr. Crawford said.

"Of course. How can I help you?"

"You and your team are doing a great thing. Christy's accident reminded me of that—of how important your ministry is."

"Did you know her?"

Mr. Crawford shook his head. "Of her. I heard about all you've been dealing with, in regard to your niece and nephew. And I read about the accident in the papers."

Noah nodded. Though he hated how quickly bad news traveled in Sage Creek, there were times when that could also prove to be a blessing, like when folks reached out.

"You've really helped clean things up around here,

broke generational addiction for a lot of families. Helped wives get their husbands back, and kids their fathers."

"I appreciate you saying that."

"My grandfather was an alcoholic. Drunk himself to death—cirrhosis of the liver."

"I'm sorry to hear that."

"It's only by God's grace my dad didn't turn out just like him, and then I probably could've, as well, but thankfully—" he rotated his wedding ring around his finger "—I never touch the stuff." He paused. "I heard about the lawsuit. Such a shame."

Seemed everyone had heard about that, not that Noah was surprised. "It is, but we'll bounce back." He didn't feel comfortable sharing more, not yet. Doing so could mess up their case. "But we have no doubt God's got this."

"Oh, I agree. You've had a lot of people praying for you, that's for sure. And it seems God's been stirring folks' hearts to help. At least, He has with this guy." He pointed a finger toward himself.

"How so?"

Mr. Crawford pulled a checkbook from his back pocket and placed it on the table. He wrote it out, tore it off, then handed it over.

Noah stared at the amount. Twenty thousand dollars? He blinked and read it again.

"I know it's not much, not nearly enough, as far as legal fees are concerned—"

"Listen—" he had to say something "—I can't say much, as this is an ongoing case, but it looks like that lawsuit isn't going to go anywhere." He tried to return the check, but the man raised his hand.

"Then I guess God was just getting me to put my money where I claim my heart is, huh?"

"This means a lot."

He smiled. "Hopefully it lets you know how much you and your ministry mean to folks. Keep changing lives, and I'll be praying that God keeps the support coming." He stood, and Noah walked him to the door, shook his hand, then returned to the table to order a slice of apple pie.

The oven timer beeped. Kayla got up to remove the banana bread, then returned to the real-estate site she'd been perusing. Not a whole lot of new construction, unfortunately. That narrowed her potential client pool, and her normal way of getting clientele. In Washington, it'd taken her three years to get on builders' call-first list, but once she had, they'd provided a steady income stream and the word of mouth she built her reputation on.

She'd practically be starting over.

Sophia began to fuss. Kayla closed her laptop and tiptoed to the kids' room, hoping not to wake Timber. Think again. He was sitting up, his favorite cloth puffy books made by Trinity Faith's quilting gals piled in front of him.

"Wead me?" He held one out.

"Read to you, huh?" She smiled, ruffled his head, then scooped up Sophia from her crib. "Hey, sweet girl." She kissed her soft head then lowered herself to the ground, back against the wall. She patted the carpet beside her. "Bring those over, little man. We should have time for a story before Uncle Noah gets here."

"No-no?" Timber looked toward the door.

"Soon." She tapped the carpet again, and after a bit, he scurried toward her, books clutched in his chubby hands. He handed over one with various animal babies on the front. *"When Farm Babies Play,"* she said, and opened to the first page. "'When farm babies play, they make all sorts of noises.' Remember, Timber?" She gave him a sideways squeeze. "'The calf says "moo."'"

He imitated her sound for sound.

"'The chicken says "Cluck-cluck." The rooster says "cock-a-doodle-doo!"'"

The hum of an engine drew closer, and tires crunched on the pebble drive. A moment later, a door banged shut and Noah's familiar booted steps climbed the stairs. She heard the front door open.

"Hey, everyone."

Timber immediately scampered to his feet. "Unca No-no!"

Kayla laughed and worked to stand with a baby in her arms. She entered the living room to find Noah hanging Timber upside down and tickling his ribs while he giggled and squirmed.

"Oh, sure." She placed a fisted hand on her hip in mock irritation. "Get them all riled up, then leave for a nice, quiet afternoon in your office."

Noah laughed and flipped Timber back onto his feet. "Guess my cover's been blown, at least, in regard to the first part. As to how I'll be spending the rest of my day, I'd kinda hoped maybe we could all hang out together. I don't have another appointment until this evening."

She smiled, her stomach giving that odd flutter it always did when his gaze landed so firmly on hers. As if she was all he could see.

Hadn't she always dreamed of having a man who would look at her like that? Who would clear his schedule just to be with her?

And Timber and Sophia. How much of Noah's behavior had to do with his love for the kids, his desire to see them raised right, and how much came from his feelings for her? Did he even know? And if she stayed, what would that look like?

What if they started dating and things didn't work out

between them? Then Timber and Sophia would experience yet another upheaval. They'd witness yet two more adult relationships ended.

But what if things worked out between her and Noah? If they managed to merge their lives, forever?

Dare she even hope?

"Man, does it smell good in here." He grabbed a paper bag he must've deposited near the door and strolled into the kitchen. "I was thinking... How would you feel about us heading outside? Hike up to the top of my property. We could bundle the kids up, bring a thick blanket to sit on and see if we can't catch a glimpse of some white-tailed deer."

She glanced out the window. It didn't seem too windy, and Timber for sure could use some fresh air. Considering the weatherman predicted rain over the weekend, they'd be wise to take advantage of the sunny day. Then again, they'd been predicting rain for almost a week now, and they hadn't seen a drop.

"That sounds lovely." She smiled. "Then after, would you mind looking at some design options I came up with for the La Conner bed-and-breakfast? We've been emailing back and forth. At first, I was confused as to what he wanted. But I think I got it figured out."

"I'm game."

"Oh, really?" She sprang to her feet. "Let's tag-team. I'll get Timber dressed. You dress Sophia." She darted off into the nursery.

Fifteen minutes and a slight temper tantrum later, they had a basket of still-warm goodies, sliced pears and juice boxes packed, and were heading toward Noah's "thinking spot," as he called it.

"I've made many a decision in that space. Spent countless Sunday evenings watching the setting sun paint the sky and talking to the One who created it."

"It sounds like a special place."

He hiked Timber onto his shoulders. "It's relaxing. Quiet." He grabbed the backpack filled with a blanket and snacks. "And beautiful, regardless what time of year it is."

They followed a dirt trail in silence, branches and pebbles crunching beneath their feet while Timber chattered on about various animals. Though most of his words still sounded a lot like babble to Kayla, she caught a few: *deer*, *horsies* and *birdies*. Less than a month ago, she probably wouldn't have even understood that, but she was beginning to learn his language—toddler speak, as Noah's mom liked to call it.

They neared the edge of the pastureland, bordered by a thicket of bare-branched trees.

Noah cast her a sideways glance. "How are things going with your sister? Any news?"

She frowned and dropped her gaze. "She's likely going to plead guilty."

"How do you feel about that?"

She scratched her eyebrow. "I have mixed feelings. I'm sad with how everything turned out, with where she's at. It wasn't supposed to be that way. When we were kids, we often played dress-up. Our mom bought us a bunch of gowns from thrift stores. One of them was white and lacy, with rhinestones sewn on. Christy always wore that one, said it was her wedding dress."

Timber ran to her clutching a handful of weeds. She dropped to his level. "For me?"

He bobbed his head.

"They're beautiful." She gave him a squeeze, took the flowers, then stood. "She had it all planned out. She always played the bride."

"What about you? Were you the groom?"

"Nope. We had a huge stuffed bear for that. I got to play the pastor, or sometimes the singer."

"Fancy."

"Oh, it was. At least, she pretended it was. By the time we reached middle school, she'd tired of that game. But she still talked about what her wedding would look like, what her life would look like. But then our parents died, and I guess she quit dreaming. I think once she quit dreaming, her hope died."

He grabbed her hand and twined his fingers through hers. "I'm sorry. I know this hurts."

"It really does. That Timber and Sophia are in this place. To see how much pain all this is causing our grandparents, not to mention that poor family that lost their husband and father." She dropped her gaze, and when she lifted it, moisture filled her eyes. "It's hard to think of my sister spending the next ten to twenty years in jail. But I'm proud of Christy for taking responsibility, for once."

"That's the first step toward freedom. Maybe this situation will be what she finally needs to get her life back together."

"I hope and pray you're right."

"Sometimes that's all you can do—hope and pray. For Christy, for your grandparents, my parents, for these little ones caught in the cross fire. I just hope none of this falls back on them, you know? That they're still able to have a happy childhood." He released a loud breath and pinched the brim of his Stetson.

"You sound worried."

He stopped at a gate flanked by trees, a field stretching behind it. With one arm securing Timber at his knees, Noah opened the gate. "A bit. I've obviously never parented kiddos before. Never really saw it done all that well, either. Least, not for most of my growing-up years."

"Not even from your mom?"

"She meant well, tried as best as she could. Most of the time, she was just trying to survive—first, my father's beatings, then doing her best to keep him from us." He winced and shook his head. "Then later as a single mom working two minimum-wage jobs just to keep food on our table and a roof over our heads. She did a mighty fine job. I'm grateful for that. But I never saw what a strong yet gentle and patient man looked like. Not until Ben."

"What about Pastor Roger?"

Noah chuckled. "Figured he didn't count, with him being so connected to God and all." He led her toward a well-trodden mount, deposited Timber on his feet, then dropped the backpack.

"So that's why you want me to stay? To help?" It stung to say it like that. Was she wrong to want more? Surely he did, too. She knew he did. She could see it in his eyes, whenever he looked her way. Whenever she caught him watching her as she read stories to Timber or puttered around in his kitchen. When he'd held her to him, both times they danced.

But did he love her enough to hold tight through whatever was ahead, the whole "sickness and health, richer and poorer," and all that?

"That's one reason," he said.

"Do you think I'd know any more than you do?" She set Sophia on the blanket he'd spread out, then helped him unload their snacks. "Prior to coming to Sage Creek, kids weren't even on my radar. Matter of fact, I was certain I'd remain single and childless forever." Partly because she'd experienced too many painful breakups, but also because she was focused on becoming the most sought-after interior designer in all of Puget Sound.

"And now?" Leaning on his side, propped on his elbow, chin in his hand, Noah studied her.

"Now…" She watched Timber tug on thick strands of grass. "Now I can't imagine a day away from these two." *Or you.*

He scooted closer, his eyes searching hers. "Then follow your heart."

Timber's wails jolted her attention, and she turned to find him facing her, crying. Palm up, he clutched his wrist with his other hand.

Still holding Sophia, she hurried to him. "Hey, buddy. What's wrong?"

Noah dashed forward and dropped to one knee, sat him on the other and inspected his hand.

"Ow!" he wailed.

"What happened?" Kayla watched over Noah's shoulder.

"Splinter. Think you can get it out with your nails?"

"I can try." And she did, but Timber only wailed all the louder and wiggled and flailed, trying to pull his hand away. "I've got tweezers back at the house." Though she hated to see this moment, when everything had been so peaceful, so…right, lost. "We should probably wash his hand, anyway, to keep it from getting infected."

The flicker of disappointment in Noah's eyes suggested he felt the same. "Good plan." He picked up Timber and held him close, and together they all returned to the house.

Unfortunately, Timber didn't sit still for the tweezers, either. "How about we give him a bath? See if we can soak the sliver out of him?"

"I'll run the water."

Thirty minutes later, Timber was a washed-and-dried, contented, wrinkled prune occupied with his miniature cars and Sophia was entertaining herself in her baby walker.

Noah poured himself a cup of coffee. "Want to go over your design ideas now?"

"Sure." She opened her computer and navigated to her documents. "He wants soft colors, primarily blue, and a rustic ocean theme. Almost like driftwood."

"Which is why he likes my furniture."

"Right."

"I found some great paintings online." She clicked to a Pinterest board she'd created specifically for this project. "This does a few things. It gives me a place to store all my finds, and makes it easy to share everything with clients. Plus, since all my boards are public, they act as advertisements."

"Smart." He eyed the images as she scrolled through.

"I loved these throw pillows." She clicked on a picture. "What do you think?"

"They're nice, but I like these better." He pointed to another set with a simpler design.

They continued going through all the items and color schemes she'd saved and narrowed them down to three different looks. "Let me figure out costs and add all this up." She dashed into the kitchen and returned with her computer bag, which she placed on the table beside her. "I should be able to get discounted prices for a lot of this stuff, if I can order them through my Washington connections." She pulled a binder from her bag, and as she did, a yellow legal pad spilled out and fell to the floor.

He picked it up, then froze, his body visibly tense. He straightened up slowly and dropped the tablet in front of her. "Kayla? What's this?"

Her hands went cold. Her notes regarding Noah's ministry. "I—I…" What could she say? *I kept a record of all the shady men hanging around your place, every blowup I witnessed, to build my guardianship case.* But she couldn't lie to him, either. She loved him too much for that, so she explained. "I was just trying to do the right thing."

"By trying to take the kids? You think that's the right thing?"

"Noah, please, you have to understand. I was worried. I just want to do what's best for Timber and Sophia."

He didn't respond for a moment. "I need some space. Please leave." He walked to the door and held it open.

"Noah, wait, please." She followed him, searched his eyes.

Sorrow filled his. He looked away, and with a heavy sigh, she left.

Chapter Twenty-Three

The next morning, Noah stretched out on the carpet to help Timber piece together a chunky wooden puzzle. Beside them, Sophia was lying on a blanket, mouthing a rainbow-colored teething ring and blowing raspberries.

He heard Kayla's soft footfalls on the front steps. He rose to meet her, getting to the door as she opened it. Dressed in pink shorts and an off-the-shoulder blouse, she looked as beautiful as ever. But sad. Based on the tiny red lines spreading from her amber irises, she hadn't slept well the night before.

"You look tired," he said.

"A little." She hiked her purse higher on her shoulder and glanced around. "Can we talk about yesterday?"

He motioned toward the couch, and she took a seat. "Coffee?" he asked.

"Yes, please."

She didn't tell him how she wanted it, nor did he ask. Because he knew. He knew how she took her coffee, her favorite flowers and ice cream, and the way she rubbed at her collarbone when nervous or deep in thought.

He knew her, but he hadn't been expecting this.

Maybe he should have. She'd expressed her concern

regarding his ministry many times. "You should have talked to me." He set a steaming mug in front of her, then sat in the armchair kitty-corner with his own mug. "How long have you been working toward guardianship?"

"It's not like that." Tears brimmed in her eyes. "I was just preparing, in case…"

"In case what?"

"I'm not trying to hurt you. You know that."

With a deep, slow breath, he nodded. He did know that. He might not like it, it might hurt like crazy, but he understood her reasons. If the situation had been reversed, he might've even done the same thing.

"So now what?" he asked.

"What do you mean?"

"You still want to take the kids?"

"I'm still worried about all the men your ministry brings around, yes. I know you're working with them, but they're addicts, which means they're unpredictable and potentially one crisis away from a relapse."

He stared at his hands. What could he say? He couldn't walk away from his ministry, nor could he lose the kids. Surely their case worker wouldn't let that happen. Like she'd said, they were doing well. This was their home—Sage Creek was their community.

"Can I bring the kids to your parents' place today? I need to stop by Trista's salon to go over some design ideas."

"So, what? That's it? Conversation over?"

"I don't know what else to say."

Neither did he, though he wished he did. He wished he knew something that would fix it all, help her feel more comfortable, or convince her to stay for good.

Lord, please show me what to do. How to make her stay.

She stood. "Drake's stopping by the salon to give an

estimate, and Trista told him I'd come to share my ideas and answer any questions he might have."

"Okay. I'll give my folks a call and let them know to expect you."

As he was helping her gather the kids' things, his phone chimed a text. He read the text, blinked, then read it again. Christy's social worker wanted to meet. Did that mean Christy had entered a plea or had been released? It seemed too soon for all of that.

Or had Kayla's take-the-kids plan progressed to the point the case worker felt the need to "talk about potential outcomes," as she called it?

"What is it?" The vulnerability in Kayla's voice squeezed his heart. But before he could answer, her phone dinged, as well. She glanced at the screen then met his gaze, her brow pinched. "Emma Jenson?"

"Yep." So the social worker wanted to meet with both of them. Probably his mom, too. "You up for it?"

She took a deep breath and nodded. "I'd say I'm available anytime, but what about the kids?"

"I'll contact Lucy. I'm sure she'll be more than happy to entertain them for a bit." He sent the text, then shot one to his parents. As he'd expected, Emma had called them, as well, and they were in the process of clearing their schedules.

Kayla's phone chimed again. She read the text, frowned and typed a response.

"Everything okay?" he asked.

"Yeah. That was my grandparents. They want me to call them."

Made sense Emma would reach out to them, too.

Within fifteen minutes, Lucy had agreed to watch the kids, Kayla was heading her way and Noah was doing his best to focus on his ministry. What if Christy was released on some sort of technicality? Or the state decided the kids would be better off with Kayla? Or she'd positioned herself for a custody battle. Could their relationship survive that? Could it survive any of this?

That afternoon, after a morning spent fretting, he arrived at the Literary Sweet Spot, their mutually agreed upon meeting place, with a heavy, anxious heart. *Lord, whatever happens, whatever direction the conversation swings, help me speak with truth and grace.*

And if, for some reason, he lost the kids? He closed his eyes against the ache welling within and reminded himself of one of his favorite childhood verses. God had promised to turn all things, even the hard and uncertain, to good. He needed to trust in that.

He shuffled to the espresso counter. "Two shots espresso. No room." He pulled out his wallet and glanced around.

Leslie took his credit card. "You looking for your mom?"

He nodded. She'd probably found someone to keep an eye on his dad and had come alone.

"They're near the back. With Kayla and her grandparents. I'm praying for y'all."

"Thank you." He took a steaming mug, then headed to a ring of overstuffed mint-and-coral-toned recliners. The circle had been widened to include three more chairs from an adjacent table.

Everyone stood to meet him. After a series of handshakes and hellos, they awkwardly stood there, shifting and glancing about.

Kayla's grandmother sat first and filled the tense silence with chatter: *How was your day? Do you think we'll get much rain this year? Our farmers sure could use it.*

Movement in his peripheral vision caught his attention, and he turned to see Emma Jenson walking toward them. She wore black slacks, a white blouse and no jewelry or makeup that he could see. "Thank you all for coming." She shook hands then sat in the vacant chair. "I spoke with Christy yesterday. She signed a waiver to terminate her parental rights."

Kayla's grandmother gasped and pressed a hand to her chest.

Noah's eyes widened. What did that mean?

"Is this final?" Kayla's grandfather asked.

Emma inched to the edge of her seat, knees pressed together. "We have a court date scheduled for early next week. But I fully expect the judge to sign off on this. Honestly, it was likely to happen anyway. She's facing some serious prison time and doesn't want the children to experience any more trauma than they already have."

"Okay." Noah leaned forward, hands on his knees. "So now what?"

Emma's gaze shifted to Noah. "Now our conversation transitions to issues related to permanency."

Noah rubbed at his thumb knuckle, swallowing back tears. Could Timber and Sophia be his? Like forever? He was almost afraid to believe it. "As in, they're up for adoption?"

"Is that something you're interested in?"

He cleared a lump lodged in his throat. "I love those rascals. I'd do anything for them."

Emma nodded, then made eye contact with the others. "You all have been doing such a great job working together. I wish all my families got along so well. It sure makes my job ten times easier." She laughed. "That said, Kayla, I do know you have some concerns."

She nodded and dropped her gaze, looking about as uncomfortable as he'd ever seen her. But then she straightened. "Like I told you when we spoke on the phone, I'm not sure I'm comfortable with the current arrangement." Her voice wobbled some.

"Are you still interested in guardianship?" Emma asked.

"Maybe."

Her words hit Noah smack in the gut.

"You can't be serious," Noah's mom said. "What does that mean? That you'd take them back to Washington State?"

"Kayla, would you move here?" Noah asked.

She appeared to struggle to meet his gaze. "I don't know. I don't think so."

His mom scoffed. "That's a lot of mighta-coulda-wantas to go about trying to disrupt a good thing. You want to stay here, help us raise those kids, fine. But don't go thinking we'll let you go carting them off halfway across the country."

"My mom's right. Timber and Sophia have a strong support system here, with all of us."

"That's not what concerns me," Kayla said.

His mom opened her mouth to speak, but Emma raised her hand. "This is an important discussion. What are your concerns, Kayla?"

She took a breath, then shared everything she'd already told Noah. "I wouldn't have a problem if they lived with Ben and Shirley—"

His mom frowned. "I'm not sure I'm up to that, not with Ben's Alzheimer's and me caring for him and all. I could watch them for an afternoon here and there, but not full-time."

"But that's the thing," Noah said. "You don't have to. That's the beauty of all of us living here, together. We can all pitch in and make sure those kids have the child-hood they deserve."

"You know the type of men Noah's ministry serves." Kayla's voice trembled slightly as she pulled a sheet of paper from her purse. It was the same page that had fallen out of her bag the day before. "We all know how unpredictable drug addicts can be. Do you really want Timber and Sophia around all that?"

"It appears we have much to work through." Emma checked her watch. "I'll talk with my supervisor and will be in touch."

The next morning, Noah meandered to the stables, looking for some quiet moments with the horses. Somehow, with their big brown eyes, the way they nuzzled their soft noses against his hand, they always calmed him. The sweat and strain of mucking out stalls didn't hurt none, either. He'd just finished cleaning one and was heading to a second when the familiar scuffle-clomp of Elliot's boots approached.

"Hey, man." Elliot stopped at the gate and draped one hand over it. "Figured I might find you in here."

"You need something?"

"Nope. Just came as a friend. The fact that we have two fresh boxes of doughnuts waiting in the kitchen and I hadn't seen hide nor hair of you said you might need one."

Noah told him about the meeting with Christy's social worker.

"No judge worth anything's going to step in and up-turn your barrels. Not now."

"I love those little rascals." A lump lodged in his throat, turning his voice husky. "Love having them around. I never wanted to be a father, and I know that's not exactly what I am here, but now..." He looked away to hide the moisture pooling in his eyes. "I don't want to lose them. Or Kayla. And from the way she was talking, it sure seems like she's already got one foot out of Texas."

Elliot nodded and rubbed the back of his neck. "What if you moved?"

"To Washington?" He shook his head. "I couldn't do that. Not to the ministry or to my folks."

"No. I mean, buy a place in town. Use this place—" he motioned in the direction of Noah's home "—as a half-way house for the men working through our program. Maybe this is God's way of lining things up. Making it so you can keep the kids and the girl."

"The way she's acting…" He shook his head.

"She's just scared. Trying to do what she feels is best for those kids. You know that."

He nodded. "I'd need a salary increase."

"That check Mr. Crawford wrote out should get us started in that direction."

A slight smile tugged on Noah's face. "True. And Kayla forwarded a contract from that La Conner business owner this morning."

"And?"

"He's down for nearly ten grand worth of furniture."

"Dude." Elliot grinned. "And I've got a feeling that's just a start."

"I hope so."

"Oh, I know so. God's opening doors right and left and will keep on opening them so long as you stay in step with Him." He clamped a hand on Noah's shoulder. "God didn't put that spark in your heart just so it could fizzle out. Trust Him and make the move. Reach out to Maddy Patella. See what properties she's got listed and for how much."

Noah smiled. "I just might do that. Matter of fact, I

might run to town now. You'll hold down the fort for me while I'm gone?"

"You know I will."

"Thanks, man. I appreciate you. Someone should give *you* a raise." If he promoted him to site director, which seemed a smart move, Noah would do just that.

"Happy to serve."

En route to his truck, Noah called their real-estate-agent friend, who happened to be free, and scheduled a time to meet up.

If he did all this, would Kayla drop her custody fight? And then what? Head back to Washington?

What would it take to make her stay?

Lord, let there be an us. *Please. I don't want to lose her.*

Once in town, he meandered through residential areas until he came to Elm Street. Maddy Patella stood waiting on the sidewalk in front of a cute little single-story house with white brick and blue trim.

Walking toward her, he tipped his hat. "Thanks for coming on such short notice."

She smiled. "Figured I owe you one, with all the properties you've helped me stage over the years." She handed him stapled papers with the home's details on the front. Three bedrooms, one bath. "This one's been on the market for six months. An estate sale."

"Sorry to hear that." He followed her up the walk to the door.

She shrugged. "It happens. The good news for you is the owner's daughter is motivated to sell."

The interior was nice. Open, with wood floors and plenty of windows. A fenced-in lawn out back would be a plus for when the kids got older. They could even get a dog. "The kitchen and bathroom are outdated but livable.

The walls need painting and the yard looks like it's been neglected for some time." Nothing he couldn't handle.

"The price reflects all that. Structurally, it's sound. Roof replaced five years ago. Relatively new furnace and air-conditioning unit."

He skimmed through the pack of papers she gave him. "All right." He flipped the pages closed and rolled them into a tube. "Let's do it."

She stared at him. "For real? Just like that?"

"Why not. Like you said, the price is good. So is the location. As to the rest, that's nothing a slow remodel can't fix." If it were just him, he'd leave it. But for Kayla… He'd get Drake to help him and they'd have the place all spiffed up in no time.

"All right. I'll call the other real-estate agent now, and we can head to my office to formalize things." She moved toward the door, opened it, then stopped. "I have to admit this surprises me. I thought you were happy where you were. What changed?"

Someone, actually three someones, had gotten a hold of his heart, that was what. So here he was, buying a house to hold on to a woman who, for all he knew, was fixing to hightail it back to the Northwest.

He was determined not to let that happen.

Once that was settled, he had one more stop. Sage Creek Jewelers. After that, Trinity Faith's monthly pot-luck, where, hopefully, he'd encounter Kayla.

And, God willing, give her every reason to stay.

Chapter Twenty-Four

Kayla deposited her design ideas, sketched out, typed and printed, on the counter of Trista's salon. Hands on her hips, she scanned the interior, then forced a smile at Drake. "Sounds like we're on the same page." She tried to focus on their meeting, but her mind kept drifting to Noah.

The man she loved. The man she'd hurt deeply.

What choice had she had? She couldn't sacrifice those kids, no matter how strong her feelings for Noah.

Trista beamed. "This is going to be so awesome! When can you start?"

"I can pick the paint colors and start finding the accent pieces this afternoon."

"Awesome." Trista turned to Drake. "What about you?"

"Same. I don't have a whole lot going on."

"Perfect." Trista shook Drake's hand, gave Kayla a hug, then walked them to the door.

Drake left with a wave.

Kayla moved to follow then stopped and turned back around. "I'm glad we're doing this. I'm looking forward to spending more time with you." That statement couldn't be more true. She'd really enjoyed reconnecting with her childhood friend. She'd miss Trista once she left. And Noah. Man, would she miss Noah. "But I'd better get going if I want to get this place snazzed up before I leave."

Trista frowned. "Don't like hearing that. And don't think we're going to let you run off that fast." She crossed her arms. "A handful of Trinity Faith ladies are interested in kitchen and bathroom remodels. Plus, Faith and Drake are having a baby."

"Seriously?"

Trista nodded. "Pretty sure they'll want help getting their nursery all set up by our very own interior designer."

Kayla laughed. "Girl, if I'm not careful, you'll have me scheduled from here till next spring."

"That's the plan."

Still smiling, Kayla shook her head and walked to her car. She paused to watch an older couple walking past, hand in hand. An image of her and Noah, some thirty years from now, flashed through her mind.

She shook away the thought. A brisk breeze swept over her, whipping her hair around her face, filling her nose with a myriad of smells drifting from the storefronts— baked goods, scented candles, fresh-brewed coffee.

Ah, coffee.

She stopped into the Literary Sweet Spot for her latte fix of the day, chatted briefly with Leslie regarding renovations she wanted to make, then spent the rest of the afternoon popping in and out of Sage Creek boutiques and antiques stores.

She paused outside the bakery, closed her eyes and inhaled, remembering a long-ago Christmas when her mom took her and Christy shopping. Old-time carols had played in every store they'd entered, and the scents of cinnamon, candles and hot cocoa filled the air. The way their mother laughed as they jokingly suggested outlandish gifts for their dad.

She'd given both of them ten dollars to spend. Kayla bought him a wallet, which he'd pretended was the best he'd seen. Christy gave him a tie and matching socks. She shook aside the memory, wishing she could do the same to the heaviness in her heart.

At 6:00 p.m., trunk loaded with various adornments for Trista's salon along with store-bought baked goods, she headed for the church for the monthly Last Sunday Dinner. Decades ago, Trinity Faith's founding pastor had started the meal as a way to care for the town's poor, and the tradition stuck.

As usual, Noah had beat her there and was standing near the dessert table, talking with a couple of men. Timber was balanced on his hip, munching on a cookie with red frosting that stained his mouth, the tip of his nose and his chubby little cheeks. Cradling Sophia, his mom sat sandwiched between Lucy and Drake's grandmother.

Noah caught a glimpse of her, and the way his face and eyes lit up warmed her from her toes.

Boy, did she love him.

Could she stay? She'd still want to get the kids away from Helping Hands and all the rough and angry men streaming in and out. Would Noah hate her for that? If she fought for custody? Would it turn ugly?

Would she lose him?

"Can you excuse me, fellas?" Noah set down Timber next to his mom. "Think you can keep an eye on little man for a minute?"

"Would love to." She placed her free arm around

Timber's back, nudged him closer and kissed his neck. "Might even have an extra cookie with his name on it."

Noah grinned. "Leave it to Grandma to get the boy all sugared up."

He wove through the crowd of people, standing in twos and threes, to Kayla.

Her eyes searched his. "Hi."

"Hey. Can we talk?"

She nodded and stood. "Sure."

"Care to go for a walk?"

"Okay."

With a hand to the small of her back, he guided her back through the living room and outside.

Dusk had fallen, and the lantern-shaped streetlights glowed against an inky backdrop and reflected on the stained-glass windows. The gravel road stretched ahead of them, flanked by trees that separated the church property from nearby houses.

He cast her a sideways glance. "I've been giving what you've said, your concerns, a lot of thought."

"Okay."

"You're right. Those kids don't need to be living so close to a place where former addicts and convicts are hanging around. But I have a solution."

Reaching the end of the road, they turned onto B Street, with its old trees, well-manicured yards and brick or paneled houses. Lights glowed in almost all of the windows.

He began mentally rehearsing his words, but they just jumbled in his head, making him more nervous.

"I'm listening," she said.

"I'm moving. Into town." He told her about the house. Her eyes widened. "Wow. That's wonderful."

"But that's not all. I bought you a little…gift."

"A gift? What for?"

He pulled a velvet box from his pocket, popped it open to reveal a wedding ring made of white gold with a single diamond glistening beneath the streetlight. "I want you to stay. With me and the kids."

Tears pooled behind her lashes. "What are you saying?"

He took her hand in his and gazed at the most beautiful woman in all of Texas. "Kayla Fisher, you are one of the smartest, kindest, most stubborn and tenderhearted women I've ever met. I never thought I could love a person as much as I do you. I'd be a fool to let you go." He slipped the ring on her finger, her soft, delicate hand trembling in his. "Will you marry me?"

She gasped and brought a hand to her mouth. "Oh, Noah. I love you."

He stood. "Is that a yes?"

"That's a yes." She wrapped her arms around him and kissed him.

Tears stung his eyes as the reality of all that had happened hit his heart with full force. And just like that, he was a family man. God had given him the kids and the girl.

Thanking Him didn't seem nearly sufficient.

Epilogue

Six months later

"I've always wanted a Christmas wedding." Kayla slipped into her satin pumps and smoothed her hand over the beaded bodice of her dress. It had once belonged to her mother, then her mother before her, modified and tailored slightly for each bride. And Noah wore cuff links that had once belonged to her father.

Somehow those two items made her feel closer to the both of them, almost as if they were here with her on this special day.

The door to the choir room opened, and Grandma swept in wearing the dress she and Kayla had picked out together. The fabric was blush-colored, belted, with a sequined bodice and shrug. The skirt extended to her ankles.

"You look beautiful, honey." She took Kayla's hands, lifted her arms, then let them drop.

"So do you. Has Grandpa caught a glimpse of you in that yet?"

Her grandmother blushed and patted the top of her hair, which Trista had curled and sprayed. "The real question is, what is that tall, handsome man of yours going to do when he sees such a vision walking down that aisle?" She patted her cheek then picked up the veil, draped over a nearby armchair.

Kayla's insides fluttered. "I still can't believe this day is here. That I'm actually getting married. Then the adoption." That was something Noah had been diligently pursuing ever since Christy relinquished her rights. After their wedding, she could do the same.

"It's crazy how God worked everything out." Her face fell, and Kayla wondered if she was thinking of Christy.

"She'll be okay. I know this is hard, but it'll give her time to kick her addictions for good." Especially if she had to serve the full fifteen years stated in her plea agreement.

Grandma nodded, grabbed Kayla's phone off a filing cabinet and snapped some photos. "Now, help me do a selfie so we can get the two of us together."

She laughed and, taking the cell, ushered her grandmother closer. "You ready?"

The door opened once again. "Hey, now." Trista came closer, waving a legitimate camera. "That there is my job, remember? The bridesmaid gets first dibs on all the candid shots. Got to show off both of your hair with all my social-media fans, after all."

Kayla smiled and circled an arm around her grandmother's waist.

Her phone rang. She recognized the number and, with a slow breath, answered. "Hello?"

"Hey, big sis. I'm so glad I was able to catch you on your big day." Thanks to Grandma and Grandpa, Christy could make calls using a prepaid debit account. "Wish I was there to hug you. I bet you look amazing."

"Thanks." A lump lodged in her throat. "I wish you were here, too. You should see little Sophia in her dress.

And Timber's in a tux. Though he's not exactly thrilled about that."

"He always had a thing with textures." She paused. "Listen, I wanted to thank you. Both you and Noah, for stepping in and taking care of those two. Timber and Sophia are fortunate to have you. I thank God for that every day."

Kayla fanned her hand in front of her face to keep tears from falling. "Thanks for saying that."

"Love you, big sister."

"Love you." She hung up and stood there, phone in hand.

Grandma came to her side and placed an arm around her shoulder. "You okay?"

"Yeah." She pressed a finger in the corner of her eye to catch a tear before it dropped and smeared her mascara. "Better than okay." And ready to commit her life—the good, the bad, the uncertain and the hard—to the man who knew everything about her and her crazy, messed-up family, and loved her anyway.

The man who promised to hold her tight and never let her go.

Watching how fiercely he'd loved both her and the kids this past year, she had no doubt he'd do precisely that.

The harp started, and Noah straightened. Shifted. Cleared his throat and shifted again. He tugged on the bottom of his tuxedo jacket, then caught a glimpse of Drake, laughing at him. As if that guy hadn't been a bundle of nerves at his own wedding.

But all his jitters left the moment he saw his beautiful bride gliding down the aisle. Her cheeks flushed slightly, and she looked at him with that same shy smile that had captured his heart just over six months prior. Her slender gown accentuated her curves, and her veil, held in place by a glimmering headband, framed the soft contours of her face.

In ten, maybe fifteen minutes, that elegant vision would be his, forever. Every morning, he'd wake to her sweet smile and soft laugh. Together, they'd enjoy walks in the park and family picnics, evening story times and living-room campouts. And at night, she'd lie beside him in the gentle glow of his bedside lamp, and together they'd talk about their day and dream about what was still to come.

Pastor Roger began with normal wedding introductions, asking all gathered to support and encourage Noah and Kayla. He knew they would. In this sanctuary, they were surrounded by family—some by blood, but most by faith. They'd walked beside the two of them this far, and Noah was certain they would for years to come.

"And now the bride and groom would like to read their vows. Noah, you're up, man."

He nodded and pulled his folded paper from his pocket and smoothed it out with sweaty hands. "I've never claimed to be good with words." Though he'd been working on what he'd say to her when the time came, for going on three months. "So I'm just going to tell it like it is. I never knew I could love a person so much. That someone could bring such joy, such light into my life. Into our lives." He motioned toward Timber, who'd become distracted from his role as ring bearer and was sitting on the carpet near the front pew instead.

"I love the sound of your laughter, and how easily it comes. The way you love Timber and Sophia, whether that means chasing after little man with a wet rag to wash strawberry juice from his face, or wearing bare patches in the carpet as you walk back and forth, trying to soothe Sophia when she's fussy. How you're so quick to see the good in others, even those who've hurt you.

"But most of all—" his voice turned husky "—I simply love you. All of you. And now I get to spend the rest of my life showing you just how much. That makes me a happy man."

"Oh, Noah." A tear slid down her cheek, and he thumbed it away. "I love you, too. Your strength, your patience and perseverance. I love that you refused to let me go and, even more, that you welcomed me into your life in the first place. There's nowhere I'd rather be at this moment, and no one I'd rather be standing here with than you. I promise to honor, respect and support you. To always be your biggest cheerleader."

"And I you."

"I promise to see the best in you and to do all I can to help bring out the best."

"I promise you the same. I'll hold tight to you, through sickness and struggle. I'll celebrate the good times with you and draw you close through the bad."

"I bind my heart to you, Noah Williams." Another tear fell and her voice quivered. "From this day forward, and only by death will we part."

"I'm not letting you go, no way, no how."

Someone near the back of the church laughed, and someone else yelled, "Yeah!"

Pastor Roger tucked his Bible under his arm. "Then by the powers vested in me by the state of Texas and this fine church body, I hereby pronounce you husband and wife. Noah, you may now kiss your bride."

He grinned so wide, he felt his cheeks stretch. Then he kissed her softly. With the joy of a man who'd finally gotten his bride.

* * * * *

If you enjoyed Building a Family,
look for Jennifer Slattery's earlier books

Restoring Her Faith
Hometown Healing

Available now from Love Inspired!

Find more great reads at
www.LoveInspired.com

Dear Reader,

Thank you for reading *Building a Family*. I hope you enjoyed getting to know Kayla, Noah and their sweet niece and nephew as much as I did as I wrote their stories. Family can be such a beautiful thing, and as I hope this story conveys, sometimes family extends beyond blood. Though the town I live in is much larger than Sage Creek, my husband, daughter and I have been able to connect with special people who have moved from mere friends to people we feel honored to walk through life with. I hope you're able to find and create such a deep community, as well.

Relationships can be hard, complicated and messy, but they can also add such beauty and richness to our lives. To those of us who are older, may we reach out to the young moms and dads among us, offering a helping hand. To those with littles still underfoot, may we never be too proud to ask for help.

And to all of us, may we find little ways to give and love and help create the type of community we ourselves long for.

Blessings,
Jennifer

COMING NEXT MONTH FROM
Love Inspired

Available June 16, 2020

AN AMISH MOTHER'S SECRET PAST
Green Mountain Blessings • by Jo Ann Brown

Widow Rachel Yoder has a secret: she's a military veteran trying to give her children a new life among the Amish. Though she's drawn to bachelor Isaac Kauffman, she knows she can't tell him the truth—or give him her heart. Because Rachel can never be the perfect Plain wife he's looking for...

THE BLACK SHEEP'S SALVATION
by Deb Kastner

A fresh start for Logan Maddox and his son, who has autism, means returning home and getting Judah into the educational program that best serves his needs. The problem? Molly Winslow—the woman he left behind years ago—is the teacher. Might little Judah reunite Logan and Molly for good?

HOME TO HEAL
The Calhoun Cowboys • by Lois Richer

After doctor Zac Calhoun is blinded during an incident on his mission trip, he needs help recuperating...and hiring nurse Abby Armstrong is the best option. But as she falls for the widower and his little twin girls, can she find a way to heal their hearts, as well?

A FATHER'S PROMISE
Bliss, Texas • by Mindy Obenhaus

Stunned to discover he has a child, Wes Bishop isn't sure he's father material. But his adorable daughter needs him, and he can't help feeling drawn to her mother—a woman he's finally getting to know. Can this sudden dad make a promise of forever?

THE COWBOY'S MISSING MEMORY
Hill Country Cowboys • by Shannon Taylor Vannatter

After waking up with a brain injury caused by a bull-riding accident, Clint Rawlins can't remember the past two years. His occupational therapist, Lexie Parker, is determined to help him recover his short-term memory. But keeping their relationship strictly professional may be harder than expected.

HIS DAUGHTER'S PRAYER
by Danielle Thorne

Struggling to keep his antiques store open, single dad Mark Chatham can't turn down his high school sweetheart, Callie Hargrove, when she moves back to town and offers her assistance in the shop. But as she works to save his business, can Callie avoid losing her heart to his little girl...and to Mark?

LOOK FOR THESE AND OTHER LOVE INSPIRED BOOKS WHEREVER BOOKS ARE SOLD, INCLUDING MOST BOOKSTORES, SUPERMARKETS, DISCOUNT STORES AND DRUGSTORES.

LICNM0620

Get 4 FREE REWARDS!

We'll send you 2 FREE Books plus 2 FREE Mystery Gifts.

Love Inspired books feature uplifting stories where faith helps guide you through life's challenges and discover the promise of a new beginning.

FREE
Value Over
$20

SPECIAL EXCERPT FROM

HQN

Sarah's long-ago love returns to her Amish community, but is he the man for her, or could her destiny lie elsewhere?

Read on for a sneak preview of
The Promise *by Patricia Davids,*
available June 2020 from HQN Books!

"Isaac is in the barn. Sarah, you should go say hello."

"Are you sure?" Sarah bit her lower lip and began walking toward the barn. Her pulse raced as butterflies filled her stomach. What would Isaac think of her? Would he be happy to see her again? What should she say? She stepped through the open doorway and paused to let her eyes adjust to the darkness. She spotted him a few feet away. He was on one knee tightening a screw in a stall door. His hat was pushed back on his head. She couldn't see his face. He hadn't heard her come in.

Suddenly she was a giddy sixteen-year-old again about to burst out laughing for the sheer joy of it. She quietly tiptoed up behind him and cupped her hands over his eyes. "Guess who?" she whispered in his ear.

"I have no idea."

The voice wasn't right. Strong hands gripped her wrists and pulled her hands away. His hat fell off as he turned his head to stare up at her. She saw a riot of dark brown curls, not straw-blond hair. She didn't know this man.

A scowl drew his brows together. "I still don't know who you are."

She pulled her hands free and stumbled backward as embarrassment robbed her of speech. The man retrieved his hat and rose to his feet. "I assume you were expecting someone else?"

"I'm sorry," she managed to squeak.

The man in front of her settled his hat on his head. He wasn't as tall as Isaac, but he was a head taller than Sarah. He had rugged good looks, dark eyes and a full mouth, which was turned up at one corner as if a grin was about to break free. "I take it you know my brother Isaac."

He was laughing at her.

The dark-haired stranger folded his arms over his chest. "I'm Levi Raber."

Of course, he would be the annoying older brother. So much for making a good first impression on Isaac's family.

Don't miss
The Promise *by Patricia Davids,*
available now wherever
HQN Books and ebooks are sold.

HQNBooks.com